AFTERHOURS

First Edition

Published by The Nazca Plains Corporation
Las Vegas, Nevada
2009

ISBN: 978-1-935509-28-8

Published by

The Nazca Plains Corporation ®
4640 Paradise Rd, Suite 141
Las Vegas NV 89109-8000

PUBLISHER'S NOTE
Afterhours is a work of fiction created wholly by *Andrew James'*
imagination. All characters are fictional and any resemblance to
any persons living or deceased is purely by accident. No portion
of this book reflects any real person or events.

Cover, Zoran Simin
Art Director, Blake Stephens

DEDICATION

First, to Brian - his boundless enthusiasm got me back on track when the scope of the tale had me overwhelmed.

Second, to the Dude and all the writers at Awesomedude, my family on the 'net..

AFTERHOURS

First Edition

Andrew James

CONTENTS

AFTERHOURS

Everyone was talking about the bashings. Jack and George, a couple who'd been together so long they'd started looking like each other, told me about Lonnie while I was losing to them at darts.

"They caught him in the park by the convention center," Jack said, throwing a perfect bull's-eye. I winced. That wasn't going to improve my already remote chances of winning. "George's friend Scott said they beat the shit out of him. When did he say it happened, George?"

"Mmm...two nights ago, I think...or did he say three?" George was usually pretty quiet and as good at darts as Jack. "Can you imagine? A harmless old man in a raincoat with a yen for sharing. The way he opened that coat was practically performance art. What kind of person could hurt someone like that?"

I grimaced and shook my head. I'd known people who'd do a lot more to someone like Lonnie than beat him, but not in this little city.

"I heard he's over at Harborview hospital. No insurance, you know. Don't you work over there?" Seeing me nod as I lined up to throw a twenty that I needed to stay in the game, he went on, "Maybe you could stop in and see him."

I hit the 14 instead, which crushed any hope I had of even making a good showing.

"Maybe I will," I said, though I knew I wouldn't.

After losing miserably, I wandered over to the pool tables. John was stretched out over the table for a tricky shot, and I paused to admire the view, as did everyone else within eyeshot. John is an ace pool player, with a scrumptious body and a sweet nature.

"Hey, did you hear about Randy?" I overheard a tall blonde ask his buddy as I watched John make the shot. "Yeah, just last night. He was coming out of Hombres and he had to piss. They caught him in the alley with his pants down. Broke his jaw in two places – fate worse than death for a blow-queen like her. Can you imagine her with her jaw wired for two months? Might as well join a convent."

I had to smile a little. I knew Randy, and it was true.

I stayed late. Chatted with John a little, and refused to play even a friendly game of pool with him. He would've felt bad, beating me the way he would have. So I listened and watched while he gave me another lesson on the finer points of pool. I'd always had a little thing for him.

And then it was time to go. Last call was announced, and I shrugged into my coat and started for home.

I have to admit, I was a little keyed up with all the talk about bashers that I'd heard. I had my umbrella poking out of my bag for a quick grab. It's got a two-foot long ice pick in the haft – yeah, it's a concealed weapon, and no, I don't have a license. So sue me.

I heard them in the alley just before the first one stepped out in front of me, so I wasn't completely surprised. Not completely, anyway.

"Hey man, got a light?" He asked, waiting for his buddies to move in behind me. I fumbled in my pocket and thought furiously. They were all big guys, with the kind of affluent, Abercrombie good looks that screamed suburban kids in the city for a little fun. They were scum in my eyes, and deserved whatever they got. But how was I going to explain to the police that one short, slightly pudgy fag took out all five? There were questions about me that I didn't want to answer. I was surprised by how irritated I was at these punks for putting me in this position. I decided to play along for now and see how the situation developed.

So, when the lead guy grabbed me and pushed me into the alley, I stumbled convincingly and screamed for help. I figured it was what most people in my position would do. In the confusion, I lost my bag – so much for my Zorro aspirations. I got up and put my back to a dumpster and squared off with the first one in the stance that I'd learned from the bare-knuckle fighters I'd trained with so many years ago. He laughed at my antique style, but when my first punch flattened his nose, he stopped laughing and snarled.

"Oh, faggot wants to fight, huh? C'mon guys, get him!"

They rushed me, and just about the time I was losing my temper and the first kick landed on my ribs, the cavalry arrived. Wonderful. Another witness.

"Hey boys, looking for a little action?" The voice from the mouth of the alley was a throaty contralto. The owner of the voice stood for a moment, backlit by the streetlight, a wisp of steam from a utilities grate winding about her ankles...it was pure theater. I couldn't help being impressed.

The bashers were impressed by the clingy black dress slit to the hip and the stiletto heels, I think.

"Go 'way, bitch – we're busy." The tall blond I'd punched knew what he wanted. I noted with some satisfaction (and a twinge of hunger) that his nose was still oozing a little blood and looking definitely misshapen.

But two of my attackers peeled off to go after her. I saw her slip out of her heels; apparently, the two closing in on her didn't see this as an ominous sign. Then things started happening very quickly.

I used the distraction to scramble to my feet, blocked another punch from the blond, and saw one of the bashers who'd gone after the girl come flying back toward us like he'd been shot from a cannon, crashing into a pile of boxes just beyond me. But it was the words the girl shouted as she took out the next one that shocked me. I'm sure that the bashers didn't recognize them, but I did, and I knew it was ok to stop playing.

I snagged the blonde's hand out of the air as he threw his next punch, twisting and snapping his wrist in one move as I slid past him. With the same hold I whipped him around, dragged him forward and kicked him in the crotch. I dropped him as I felt a blow on the side of my head that left my ear ringing and spun to face the next one. I let myself go a little: bared my teeth and growled at him. He screamed and tried to run, but I swept his legs and kicked him in the head, putting him out for the duration.

I looked around for the last one. He was trading kicks and punches with the girl about ten feet away. I scooped up a board from under the dumpster and slugged him with it from behind. He went down without a sound.

We stood there a moment. The girl was not a girl. Sometime during the scuffle, his wig had come off. It lay in the filthy alley, looking like someone had stepped on it. Several times.

"You ok?" I asked.

"Never better. I think I've ruined these stockings, though. They're silk. You owe me."

"Let's go, right now. I don't want to see them anymore." I could feel the desire growing in me. It was time to go.

We called the police from a pay phone. Then Sandy, my fair rescuer, agreed to allow me to buy him breakfast – as a first installment on the stockings, you understand.

Mike's is a twenty-four hour diner, with cute waiters and some pretty fine breakfasts. Everett was the lead waiter that night, so the music was deep, soulful blues. We took a booth toward the back.

"You handle yourself pretty well in a scuffle." I commented, as we each perused the menus.

"Once you got started, you did ok too…what were you waiting for, the cavalry?"

"Who'd have thought the cavalry would arrive wearing a wig? By the way, does that go against my account too?" The much-abused wig had taken up residence in a dumpster just before we left the alley.

"That old thing? That why I rushed to the rescue: I was hoping that wig wouldn't survive."

I laughed and Everett arrived with breakfast: my usual mocha and toast, and a vegetarian omelet, hash browns and orange juice for Sandy. I nibbled my toast and sipped my coffee while I watched Sandy eat for a few minutes. I love watching people eat, and Sandy was more interesting than most. He ate with small, efficient bites, everything cut neatly and deftly, and with frequent dobbings with his napkin.

"I hadn't heard anyone yell that particular phrase in a fight in a long time," I said casually as Sandy paused for a sip of orange juice. His eyes widened as he looked at me, and I was impressed that he didn't choke on his juice.

"Um...what phrase? Oh, you mean that back in the alley?" He was the picture of casual indifference, but I'd seen the momentary surprise.

"Uh-huh. Where'd you learn that, anyway?"

"Oh, just something my mother taught me...she said it distracted people in a fight."

"Ah, then your mother was the armsmistress?"

"Why, yes...err, no, I mean...maybe I'd better be going...."

I rested my hand on his wrist, not hard enough to stop him if he really wanted to go. "Stay, please. I didn't mean to make you uncomfortable. It's just that you're new in town – because I *know*

I'd have heard of you if you weren't – and it's a small community, and I'm just curious about you."

"Well, don't be. I'm just a small town boy from Pennsylvania."

"Really? What part? I have relatives all over that area…"

"Uh…"

"I'm going to show you something Sandy, something that I never show most people. But I have a feeling you're not 'most people.'" With that, I let my fangs descend and my eyes burn red, the demon that burned within me staring out for a moment. I continued, "Yes, I'm a member of the Kin, Sandy, though some of your people would disagree. I think you are too. You're a long way from Elf-hame, the land underhill."

Sandy was clearly shaken, but he smiled bravely. Our kinds were traditionally deadly enemies, but he was a sidhe alone and far from home. For a moment, he let his glamour slip, trading trust for trust.

His chin was sharp and narrow, and his cheekbones could have cut glass. Sharp, pointed ears rose behind each temple, and his hair was thick and glossy black. His eyes were tilted at the outside corners and the pupils were slits like a cat's. He was inhumanly beautiful.

Then the mask slid back into place and he was just an attractive young man in a dress, wearing too much makeup.

"So welcome to town, Sandy."

He laughed. "Why, thank you. Are there many of us around?"

"Oh yeah, we're everywhere. Seely and Unseely alike, we pretty much give up all that when we come out, and just try to get along in the community."

"Makes sense to me. Never did like all that 'traditional enemies' stuff anyway."

"So what are you doing tomorrow night?"

"Taking my second payment on those very expensive stockings, I hope."

I smiled, and sipped my mocha.

Cultural Differences

It was another Friday night at the bar. I was flying solo tonight because Sandy was doing his regular gig over at the dance bar – a little variety show thing where all the dancing queens sat on the floor and watched him dance and sing his ass off. In the six weeks since I'd met him, he'd become the latest and greatest talent to hit the drag circuit. How he managed to dance in 8"stiletto heels was beyond me, but he did it as well as he did everything else. The boy could have given the fabulous Miss Turner a run for her money. And instead of the usual lip-synching, he sang everything he performed in a voice that would have made Maria Callas flush with envy. He'd promised to come over when he was done "entertaining the troops" as he called it.

So I was hanging out by the wall, just taking in the view and enjoying a little cold beer (yes, even I enjoy a little microbrew on occasion). Jack and George were beating the pants off a young college boy at darts, Ted was behind the bar chatting up a cute young thing I saw come in with the college boy, and all the regulars were playing pool. Except, I noticed suddenly, John.

Usually it would have taken a pool cue to the head for John to quit playing, but tonight he was sitting off to one side, drinking beer after beer and not even signed up for a table. I could almost see the black thunderclouds gathered over his head. Most unusual. So, I sauntered over to where he was seated on a stool next to the wall. I noticed he was a little wobbly on the stool. John isn't usually much of a drinker.

"Hi, John. You look like someone just ran over your cat. You ok?"

I saw him stiffen up, and then he wheeled around on the stool and grabbed the front of my shirt in both hands and jerked me up close to his face.

"What do you know about my cat, asshole?" he growled, the beer on his breath blasting me in the face.

"Whoa, easy big fella. I don't know anything about your cat. Did something happen to it?"

His face went from snarling hatred to sad and pathetic little boy in a split second. He grabbed me and hugged me hard.

"Oh Ralph (that's me, by the way, and it's pronounced 'Rafe,' thank you very much) some son of a bitch killed my cat!" And he broke down in my arms, sobbing his heart out into my shoulder. To say I was a little surprised doesn't even touch it. John is always a lighthearted, easygoing kind of guy. I'd never seen him even annoyed, much less as utterly heart-broken as he seemed to be. I held him and let him cry for a little while.

"I'm so sorry John...why don't you tell me what happened?"

"I can't talk about it here…nobody here cares about anything except goddamn pool and their next lay. You're the first person who's even come up and asked me what's wrong all night."

"You know everyone here cares about you, John. Maybe they're just a little preoccupied with what they're doing."

"Yeah, some friends," he said bitterly through his tears.

"Come on then. Let's go to Mike's and get a booth in the back and you can tell me what happened, ok?"

"Aw, I don't want to ruin your night with my problems…"

"John. This is me. I'm your friend, and I have been for a long time. You know I don't play pool and I don't get laid. What else do I have to do?" I smiled at him and got a wan little smile in return. He nodded and slid off his barstool, his arm still around my shoulder. I picked up his jacket, balanced him with my other arm as he swayed dangerously, and then steered him to the door.

Outside, I sat him at one of the little tables on the sidewalk that get used when the weather is warmer.

"I need to call Sandy and tell him we're going to be at Mike's," I said. "Is it ok if he joins us?"

"Umm, yeah." He put his head in his hands and sat while I fumbled in my pocket and pulled out my cell phone-handy little devices they are, too; One of the best things about this day and age.

"Hi Sandy, it's me. You all done over there?" I could hear the thumping of dance music over the cell.

"Yup. The kids are back on the floor shaking their groove thangs. What's up?"

11

"John's feeling a little under the weather over here, so we're going to Mike's for a cup of coffee. You wanna join us?"

"Sure, that'd be great. My legs are killing me. If you get there before I do, order me a red apple martini, won't you? I'm parched." Sandy had just discovered the red apple Martinis at Mike's and they'd become the drink du jour.

"You got it. See you up there in a few minutes." I hit the 'end' button and put the phone back in my pocket. It was a bit of a walk to Mike's, and I figured a little fresh air wouldn't hurt John a bit.

"Hey, what's up with you and Sandy, anyway? You two have been awfully buddy-buddy since he showed up." John seemed to be doing a little better once we started walking.

"Oh well, you know, just good friends and all that. Always a bridesmaid, never a bride-that's me."

"That's fucked up, Ralph. You're the nicest guy I know… just like tonight, you taking time to take me to coffee. A nice guy like you shouldn't be alone."

"No-one should be alone unless they choose to be John, but lots of us are. It's the way of the world."

"That is so true! No one ever falls in love with me. They just take me home and want to screw me, and then it's out the door before their boyfriend gets home. I'm too old for that shit," he said drunkenly.

"You have no idea," I muttered, and kept walking with his arm looped through mine. I hoped desperately he wouldn't remember this conversation tomorrow.

At Mike's, the lights were low and the oldies were playing on the sound system. When I say 'oldies' I don't mean eighties disco, I'm talking big bands here. Everett saw us come in and hustled over to greet us, leading us to a booth in the back. Not many people know it, but I'm a partner in the business. Years ago there wasn't an all night diner on the Hill, so I'd approached Mike about starting one. He ran the show and I pitched in the financial backing. If you live as long as I have, money usually isn't an issue.

I poured John into the booth and slid in on the other side. Everett gave me a warm smile.

"Right," he said, "One giant black coffee for your friend and the usual mocha for you. What else can I get you, Ralph?"

"Bring us one of those red apple martini thingies, Ev. Sandy will be joining us in a few minutes, I think." Everett made a comical face of distaste and rolled his eyes. He shared my disapproval for calling anything that sweet and...well, red...a martini.

Sandy showed up a few minutes later, gorgeous as always in a chocolate brown burnt velvet gown with an asymmetrical hemline and his trademark heels. He flopped into the booth and looked at John trying to sip his coffee without burning his lips.

"Hi John...been dipping your head in a beer barrel? You look like hell, man."

"Thanks," he grunted sourly and continued to nurse at his coffee.

"Drink your martini thingie and hush, dear. John is going to tell us what happened to make him try to drown himself in a pint glass."

"I'm all ears," he said and grinned at me. I think I managed to stifle my laugh…mostly.

"If you two are through clowning around…" John was looking a little irritable. Neither one of us answered, just gave him our undivided attention.

"Well," he said miserably, "it started early this week, on Tuesday. I came home from work and my landlord mentioned that her dog was missing. She told me that the neighbors on each side had complained of the same thing. I told her I'd keep an eye out, but that Kitsura – it's one of those Japanese dogs that looks like a fox, y'know – would probably be home soon and not to worry too much. I didn't think much more about it. Then I got home on Wednesday, and I found out what happened to Kitsura and the neighbors' dogs. When I got home, I found their heads on my front porch, stacked in a perfect pyramid. That was pretty horrible, guys. I called the police and my landlord was devastated, and it was really bad."

"Yeah, I could see that being a pretty bad thing. So what did the police say?"

"Not much. No suspects, no evidence of any kind…just three dog heads on my front porch."

"Mmm, freaky. I'm so sorry John. That really sucks." Sandy looked at John with real concern in his eyes.

"Then, I came home on Thursday, and….and…"he ground to a stop and sobbed. "I came in the house and Gilly didn't meet me at the door like she always does. I started looking for her, and I looked out the window and something was hanging on a branch outside. I looked closer and it was…oh god…Gilly. Someone had pulled her skin off and left her hanging on a branch outside my window. Why Ralph? She was just a little cat, but I loved her. Why did they do that to her?" Tears ran down John's face as he stared at me, demanding answers I didn't have.

Sandy got up and slid into the booth beside John, wrapping him in a tight hug. "Jesus honey, I'm so sorry that happened to you. It's horrible…"

We left shortly after that, took John home and put him to bed. When he wasn't looking, Sandy wove a sleep spell over him to exclude all dreams and to last 8 hours. He was snoring before we let ourselves out the door, locking it behind us. Sandy set a ward spell on the door, also to last 8 hours. If anyone tried the door before then with malicious intents, they were in for a big surprise. I've always envied elves their magical abilities.

"So what are we going to do?" Sandy asked. "Don't look at me like that. You know we have to do something."

"Did you happen to notice the smell in John's apartment?" I asked. "I thought I smelled a very faint odor in there. I think one of our kind is involved."

"It wasn't an elf. None of us would do that. If John had somehow offended one of us, he'd have been challenged to a duel."

"Right. And another vampire would have just killed him and made a snack out of him. So it wasn't either of our kind directly. But I'd bet anything you'd care to name that something fey is behind all this."

"Tempting offer, but I think that's a bet I'll turn down. But we can't do much till we know what we're looking for, and I'm fresh out of inspiration. What should we do?"

"I think," I said slowly, "as much as I hate to do it, I think we need to talk to Gideon."

"Who's Gideon? What would he know about all this?"

"Not as much a 'who' as a 'what'. He owns a bar downtown. Really nice guy, but he makes me a little nervous."

"Whoa. Pretty big mojo if he makes you nervous," Sandy teased.

"Absolutely. The biggest. Not many of our kind walk into his bar at all, and even fewer leave without pissing their pants along the way somewhere."

"Ah. So what makes him such a big cheese?"

"He's an angel."

"Oh. Oh, I see. Umm, what's he doing owning a bar in this little burg?"

"He tells me he got sick of it and retired."

"I didn't know they could retire."

"They can't."

We didn't say much else till we got back to my place and picked up my beat up old Volvo wagon. A few minutes later we pulled up in front of Gideon's Spirits, a bar just off Second on Battery Street. It looked pretty much like any other dive along this street, to the mortal eye – neon beer signs lit up, and bars over the tiny windows. Drunks hate sunlight almost as much as I do.

But to immortal senses, the place fairly radiated power. The windows shone with blue radiance and there was a deep sense of peril that permeated the air around the whole place. Sandy took one look and paled. I simply nodded grimly and parked the car.

"We're going…in there?" Sandy squeaked.

"Uh-huh. Don't worry; I'll pay the cleaner's bills. Oh, by the way – your glamour won't work in there. Don't sweat it – they'll all see what they're supposed to see. But I'd take it off right inside the door. Gideon thinks it's discourteous to come in disguised."

With that I took his hand and we stepped into Gideon's Spirits.

Now unmasked, we walked down a short hall and into the main bar. There were a number of people sitting at the bar, and more at the tables. Inside it looked like a dive too, except for the omnipresent waves of power that radiated through the room. Sandy, being of Seely Court, wasn't as bothered by it as I was. I just wanted to howl and run out of the place as fast as I could, but I held on and walked to the bar.

Gideon looked like a biker. A really big biker, I might add. He stood at least six inches over six feet, had long black hair pulled into a pony tail and a big beard. His arms were as big as my thighs, and his neck almost as big. Of course he'd seen us come in.

"So Ralph, welcome back. You don't come see me nearly often enough. Who's your friend? Wait, let's see if I can guess: Sir Sandellifer, late of Dusksong Hame. Not your usual type, Ralph. What brings such an odd couple to my bar?"

"Hey Gideon, how you been?" I keep my comments to Gideon as short as possible, for fear that I'd blurt out just how nervous he made me. Truth was, he made me want to confess all the terrible things I'd ever done, and I'd have ended up being here all night: Sins of a misspent youth and all that.

"So, what can I do for you boys?" Gideon was always pretty direct, which made this whole thing a lot easier. Visiting him

17

is still the hardest thing I ever do, but at least he doesn't prolong the agony.

Sandy glanced at me and saw how pale I was looking, and launched into our tale. He kept it short and sweet and to the point. I could have kissed him.

"Hmm.... interesting. And this John doesn't ever remember ever doing anything that might piss someone off? No-one who might be interested in hiring a little fey muscle as paybacks?"

"No sir," Sandy stated. "He's the nicest guy on the planet. I don't think he's had an enemy in his entire life."

"Let me think a minute. There's something about this that sounds familiar...let me go get that guy down there a beer. Be right back."

The pressure of his presence dropped a little as he walked away down the bar to get another patron a beer. I sighed and slumped, dropping my head into my hands, my elbows braced on the bar.

"Are you going to be ok?" Sandy asked.

I swallowed a throatful of bile and nodded without looking up. Every evil thing I had ever done played across my vision on the back of my eyelids, some almost enough to make me throw up. I'd changed, dammit! I wasn't the person who had done those things. I gathered myself and sat back up as Gideon came back down the bar toward us, a thoughtful look on his face.

"Ok gentlemen, I think I've got it. But let's talk prices first."

Sandy glanced at me and I nodded. There was always a price for information from Gideon. Always worth the price, of course-his tips were always right on the money.

18

"Here's what I need from you two. Since there are two of you, you're each going to pay, got it?"

I nodded. It was the way Gideon worked.

"Ralph, a situation has come to my attention that I think you could help me with. There's a young man that lives in the north end, up along Lake City Way. He's not a nice boy, Ralph. He lives a few blocks away from a junior high school, and he's gotten some of the kids there hooked on meth. First he gives it to 'em for free, and then he starts charging 'em. When they can't pay, he starts 'em on a barter arrangement. Know what I mean? No kid should have that happen to 'em. I think a visit from you might help him see the error of his ways. Don't kill him, but don't be afraid to get a little rough with him. I don't think a little blood loss would hurt him either. His name is Dan Harrelson. Don't worry about reporting back when it's done. I'll know. I'd like this expedited, if you don't mind."

I nodded. It was the kind of payment I didn't mind making.

"Now, as for you, Sir Sandellifer. I hear you're quite the chanteuse. I hope that voice of yours isn't all glamour, because I'd like to beg a couple hours of your time and talent. It's been a very, very long time since I sang duets with anyone that could keep up, and even longer since I sang with the sidhe. That's what I need from you."

Sandy was clearly taken aback, but his years of court training stood him in good stead. He stood and bowed, deeply and formally.

"It would be my honor and my pleasure, Gideon. Pray, where and when shall this most welcome event occur?"

Gideon laughed. "Oh, very prettily spoken, Sir knight. Never fear, I will contact you within the week on time and place. I think we'll make some very pretty music together."

"I am at your service and shall strive to my utmost, Gideon."

He smiled and nodded. "Now, as to the information you needed. I shan't tell you who is responsible or why these things have happened to your friend, but I'll tell you where you may find the answer. You are correct in thinking that this is a problem involving a fey being. I wouldn't be surprised if you were to find the answers you seek in a buried garage on Twelfth avenue east, just south of Republican. Look on the east side of the street behind a large, beige house. I leave the means of resolving the problem to the two of you, for I think you are uniquely qualified to understand and resolve it. I advise mercy in dealing with what you shall find- this is a misunderstanding, nothing more."

I nodded, thanked Gideon and started for the door as quickly as I could without being impolite.

"Oh Ralph, one more thing." I turned and looked at the enormous man behind the bar. "You are indeed a changed being. The past is the past, and shall not be held against you. Go in peace."

I nodded, and walked quickly down the hall, followed by a bemused Sandy. There was a gray light in the east when we hit the street, so I dropped off Sandy at his apartment, and after agreeing to meet him the next evening to explore the answer we had gotten from Gideon, I went home and slept like the dead.

The next evening, a couple hours after sunset, I paid a visit to a certain apartment on Lake City Way, and had a little chat with a certain someone there. I acquainted him with a few facts concerning his continued survival, and obtained his promise to

20

lead a blameless life from here forward. It was a most satisfactory discussion, and when I left, this someone was looking a little pale and shaken. I understand that being a pint or two shy of blood can have that effect though. I made sure he understood that his actions would be monitored in the future, and thoughtfully advised him to drink some orange juice and eat a few cookies before I left him.

I later heard that certain parents of children who attended the nearby school received anonymous phone calls informing them of some rather disturbing activities on the part of their children, and several children were said to have started in drug rehab and counseling sessions as a result of these calls.

It was just about Midnight when I met up with Sandy. He was looking pretty casual in worn blue jeans and a tight black tee. I was wearing pretty much the same thing, except I had my favorite black leather jacket on.

"Why Sandy, I didn't even know you owned boy clothes," I teased.

"You're looking pretty butch yourself tonight, big boy. Expecting trouble?"

"You know what I know, darlin'. I think we'll be able to handle whatever it is, though. Gideon wouldn't send us into a situation he didn't think we could handle."

"Shall we walk?" Sandy smiled and looped his arm through mine, and we walked up Twelfth Avenue that way, a short pudgy leather daddy and a tall, beautiful twink. No one paid us the slightest notice.

Just south of Republican, we found the house as described. It was one of those old, giant houses that has been partitioned into apartments, and it butted up against a tall embankment in the back…a brick wall covered with ivy, it turned out. The smell of something fey was strong back there, and I noticed a couple of windows about eight feet up from where I stood on the sidewalk. When I looked back from the windows, I saw that Sandy had dropped his glamour and was standing beside me in full Sidhe battle array: silvery armor and greaves, a light helm on his head and dripping with chain mail. An enormous sword was sheathed in a baldric on his back. Pretty imposing, I have to say. I nodded in satisfaction, but couldn't help but needle him a little.

"So you actually know how to use that pigsticker?"

He looked at me down his nose-not especially difficult for him, as he had about three inches on me.

"I have some passing knowledge of its use. You do your part and try not to get in the way, right?" His voice was deeper and more formal than I was used to from him, but I heard the laugh behind the words. I nodded, and turned to look at the windows again, and noticed that a pane was missing in the left hand one. I pointed it out.

"I'll go in through there, and open the window from the inside. I won't be able to see anything when I get in there, so I won't know if anything is in there with me. Be ready to get in there quick if I get jumped. Got it?"

Sandy nodded, and I did one of the best tricks a vampire can do. I dissolved into a thin, white mist and drifted up to the window and through the missing pane. It was a good thing it was a still night…I'd known more than one of my kind that has been permanently dissipated by an unexpected breeze.

I reformulated right below the window in a crouch, which was a good thing, because something big and solid came flying out of the dark right through where I would have been standing. It crashed into the wall opposite and bounced back to it's feet and was on me in a heartbeat. I punched hard for where I hoped its nose was and it grunted and grabbed me. I managed to hold it off, but the damn thing was trying to bite me, so I tried to push it back, but it was too strong. Then the glass in the right hand window blew inward and Sandy cannonballed into the room, with that giant pigsticker in hand and glowing all over like a Christmas tree. The point of his sword snaked past me over my shoulder and ended up about an inch from the face of my opponent, and he froze.

"Yield varlet, or your life is surely forfeit." Sandy's voice was icy cold and full of menace. I was glad he wasn't talking to me. In the light of Sandy's armor, I saw what I'd been wrestling: big, solid muscle, with an enormous mouth full of jagged triangular teeth and wearing a red hat. Shit! No wonder I'd had so much trouble… I'd been wrestling a Redcap.

"I yield, knight." Its voice was deep and gravelly, but I sensed an uncertainty in its voice. "My life is yours till you depart this place, on my word of honor." I was a little rusty on the forms, but that sounded unusual to me. Still, it seemed to satisfy Sandy, who withdrew his sword and sheathed it in a single move. The Redcap let go of me and just like that it was over. Yeah, I know: kind of weird but that's how business is done between Seely and Unseely.

"I would know the name of he to whom I have yielded, Sir knight. It is my right," the Redcap stated a little defensively.

"Know that I am Sandellifer, lately a knight of Dusksong Hame and now of this place. Whom is it my privilege to address?" A little formal, I know… but this was all part of the ancient forms.

"I am called Undone, for I am dead though I breathe and walk."

"Wight, where is your motley? Wherefore are you in this place alone?" Sandy's voice had warmed a little, and he seemed genuinely curious.

"I have no motley, noble sir, for I have been cast out and my life is over, though to my shame I cannot end it myself. If I may ask a boon, honored knight: please, kill me. I must die but I cannot perform this act myself, to my eternal shame." And the Redcap burst into tears and threw himself on the floor at Sandy's feet.

I looked at Sandy's face, and he looked even more astonished than I felt. You see, Redcaps are pack animals, much like dogs or wolves, and their family group is called their motley. Their total devotion is to the motley. A lone Redcap is a contradiction in terms. They're tough, they're mean, and it's a damn good thing I didn't let this one bite me, because he'd have take my arm off at the shoulder and come back for three more bites to get the rest of me. So to see one groveling and crying was a bit of a shock. What had bothered me about his oath of peace earlier, I realized, was that he hadn't sworn on his motley's honor, only on his own. This was getting weirder and weirder.

Sandy knelt next to the miserable Redcap and spoke gently. "Come, good Wight. Let us speak of this crime that has so precipitously ended your life. Know you that my good companion is Ralph Von Aarenstadt. We would hear your tale and know what has brought you to this pass."

"You would be kind to me, whom you have vanquished? But I am Unseely, and you are of Seely Court. Why do you not slay me, good sir?"

"I do not slay without reason, and wherefore have I reason when all you have done is defend your hold against invaders? Surely that is your right?"

"I no longer know what is right, good knight. I have lost all ability to reason. I am mazed and whelmed by what has befallen me, and I know not where or to whom I may turn."

"Tell me your name from before you were exiled. I shall not call you Undone, for I do not believe it to be true. Let us talk of this thing."

"I was called Slider, of the Holly Park motley before my shame, sir."

"Good. You may call me Sandy, and my companion Ralph. So, tell us how it is that you come to be here alone."

"Sir Sandy, I was taken with a kind of madness. I cannot explain it. My life was turned upside down. I cannot eat, my stomach flutters like a butterfly, and I feel great happiness and then deepest pain and sadness almost on top of one another. I watched him from afar for so long, and I was happy that he was alive and in the world, but I knew I could not be with him and I felt a terrible pain like a bite in my chest." He was gasping and crying a little as he spoke, and I could feel his misery. This poor thing was in a world of hurt.

"Slider, if we leave here, can we agree not to fight each other?" I asked. "I think you need a chance to tell your tale to us, but I'd kind of like to hear it over a nice mocha. What do you think, Sandy?"

"I will accept Slider's word of honor on it, Ralph. I think he is honorable. What say you, Slider? No harm to each other till we agree otherwise? You have my honor as a knight upon it."

"I have nothing to lose, Sir Sandy. If you will it, it is done on my word of honor."

"Excellent. C'mon then, let's go to Ralph's place. It's closer than mine."

Back at my place, I made myself a mocha, passed on of my 'guest beers' to Sandy and knowing Redcaps as I do, put some ice in a pint glass and poured a full glass of Windex over it. I could have given him Drain-O, but I didn't want him drunk.

When he saw the glass I handed him, Slider looked a little puzzled, then sipped it and smiled for the first time since I'd met him.

"This is wondrous brew, Ralph. What is it called?"

"Umm, we call it Windex. I'm glad it's to your liking."

"So, let's hear it, Slider. What happened to you?"

"There is a man, Sandy. A human, who lives not far from here. I first saw him three months ago, when I was out foraging. It was the first time I was allowed out by myself. He walked by the alley where I was hiding, and never saw me. I have seen many humans in my life; the motley keeps some to help with chores and things, so that was nothing new. But there was something different about this one. He walked proudly, with his head up and looked strong and powerful, though I know humans are weak things and easily broken. I watched him pass and I went about my business, but something about him called to me, in some strange way. I ignored it and found food and went home.

"That night I dreamed of him. He strode through my sleep like a storm, carrying all before him. I saw him defeat the motley, and when it came my time to fight him, I could not. Instead I swore myself to him. But this was just a dream and I ignored it and went on about my business. Only I began to forage only in this neighborhood, and found myself watching for his comings and goings, and I learned where he lived and watched him. Soon

26

I forgot to forage and only watched him. He never saw me, but I knew him. And I fell into this strange madness, as I told you before."

"How old are you, Slider?" Sandy gently asked.

"I turned thirty a fortnight agone."

"That's very young for your kind, isn't it?"

"I am a man, full grown. But yes, I am almost the youngest in the motley."

"I see. Have you been with a woman of your kind?"

The Redcap blushed. "No sir. There was a woman of a different motley that had spoken for me, but I didn't..." his voice trailed off.

"I understand." Sandy looked at me, and I shrugged. He seemed to be doing fine. "So what happened then?"

"The Alpha got very mad at me. He beat me and told me I must find food while I was out foraging or the motley would starve. So I worked hard and I brought food back, but I suffered because I didn't see this man. It was very hard, because I knew I had to work for the motley, but my mind was only for this man. And then..." Slider stopped and slumped in the chair. He blushed again and took a deep breath, and then went on. "I realized that I wanted this man for my mate. I know... it is very sick and I am a verminous thing for wanting it, but it's true."

I was astounded, though I guess I should have seen where this story was going. I gaped at the Redcap, but Sandy didn't seem phased.

"Allow me to interrupt and to tell you something, Slider. There is a reason why I am in this place and not in my home Underhill. I, too, desire the love of males, and I think you are not sick at all."

An elbow in the ribs from Sandy snapped me out of my shock and I joined in.

"Me too, Slider. There is nothing wrong with loving another man. Some of us are just like that, you know. It's part of who we are. But continue your story. What happened next?"

"Well... once I knew this, there was only one thing to do. I went to his hold and left him a promise gift. Isn't this what everyone does when they want someone to be their mate?"

A horrible thought hit me at that moment. Oh God, please tell me it isn't so!

"Umm... so what kind of gift did you leave, and where did you leave it?"

"A promise of food, of course. I left him the heads of three animals in front of his door to prove to him that I would be a good provider, and that he would never go hungry if he were my mate. This is how it is done... even I know this." He was giving me a look like I was a total idiot for not knowing.

"Anything else?" I choked out.

"Yes," he said proudly. "I went into his hold, and found a small animal he had captured and skinned it out and hung it where I knew he would see it, to prove that I was skilled at preparing food as well as hunting."

Oh shit. I looked at Sandy and saw that he'd figured it out as well.

"Slider, I need to talk to Sandy in the other room for a moment. You stay here and enjoy your drink and we'll be right back, got it?"

"All right, Ralph." He had a puzzled look on his face but relaxed back into his chair and sipped his drink.

I grabbed Sandy and hauled him off to the bedroom and shut the door. We looked at each other in total panic.

"Jesus Christ on a fuckin' bicycle, Ralph! I thought you said Gideon wouldn't send us into a situation we couldn't handle?"

"Yeah, that's what I thought," I spat angrily. "I can hear that bastard laughing all the way up here from downtown."

"What the hell are we going to do, Ralph? He's just a kid, and he's in love with John. He'll die if we don't help him."

"What the fuck do you want us to do, Sandy? This kid could eat a car for dinner. He thinks a sharpei is a snack, for Christ's sake."

"I don't know, I don't know.... I have to think. What can we do?"

"Okay, okay. So we've decided we're going to help this kid? This means we're responsible for what happens, right? So we have to do this right."

"Right. So what are you thinking?"

"Well. If we didn't help this kid, he would die. Why?"

"Because he doesn't have a motley. Why? Are you going to find him one he can join? I don't think it works that way. They're family based... oh."

"Yeah. Oh is right. You really want to help this kid? Okay then. How far are you willing to go?"

Sandy turned away and walked to the window, and stared out for a minute. When he turned back, I saw that he'd made up his mind.

"I'm in if you're in."

"Okay then, let's go tell him."

Back in the living room, Slider was sitting in the chair and looking sad and dejected again. He looked up when we came in, and the look on his face was enough to break my heart, which I'd thought long past the breaking stage. Sandy and I walked up in front of his chair and he slid forward onto his knees in front of Sandy.

"Please sir…Sandy. Now you know why I begged a boon of you when first we met, and now I must ask if you will grant it. I must die, and I cannot kill myself. You must do this for me… please."

"No. I deny you that boon. I will not do it."

The Redcap's face fell even further, if that was possible. He wearily dragged himself to his feet and spoke simply.

"Very well. I shall go back to my cave and die there. At least I will be close to the man who has brought me to this when I die. I thank you for your kindness, Ralph. I will take my leave."

"Slider, wait. We have something that we'd like to ask you. Sort of a counter-boon, if you will. You see, Sandy and I are a motley. We look out for each other, and take care of each other. Only we're not very strong with just two of us. We need a strong third man with us to be strong enough to survive. Someone we trust to watch our backs, and uh… help us gather food and things like that. We want you to join our motley."

It stopped him in his tracks. He looked like someone had just hit him in the middle of his forehead with a twelve-pound sledgehammer. He gaped at us for a moment, then managed to get a few words out.

"But… but motleys are family. You can't have a motley… you're not even related."

Sandy cut in. "But we are. We're brothers by adoption. Only we adopted each other, instead of someone else adopting us."

"Slider," I said, "Sandy and I are both outcasts too. Our kinds don't like us much because we want other men to be our mates. So we pulled together a motley of our own, because we care about each other, even if we're not related by blood."

"And… and you want me to join your motley? You would adopt me and make me your brother too?" The look on his face went from confusion to joy and back in seconds. "But where would we have our camp? I've been all over this hill and there is no place for us."

"Well, Slider, we do things a little differently than your old motley. You know that I live here, in this place. And Sandy has a place where he lives too. It's not very far away. So we don't live together like your old motley did."

"But that's not right. A motley lives together, Ralph. I don't see how this works."

"We plan on finding a place where we can live together, don't we. Ralph? A house, right Ralph? And we were planning on doing that real soon and we want you to move in and live with us, right Ralph?" Sandy was laughing at me with his eyes, daring me to disagree.

"Umm...right! That was the plan. We're looking for a house..."

"It's strange to me, but I think it will work. So we will be a motley." The smile on Slider's face was worth all this sudden change. Did I mention that I hate change? Well, I do.

"But what shall we call our motley?"

"The Three F's motley of course."

Slider suddenly reached forward and swept us into his arms, hugging us close against his enormous chest. Redcaps are not known for the quality of their personal hygiene, and the smell this close to Slider was fairly breathtaking. In between gasping for breath, I managed to ask a question.

"Sandy...the three F's? What does that mean?" I winced, almost hating to ask the question.

"Freaks and Fags Forever, baby!"

It was the hardest thing I've ever done. Imagine housebreaking and training a 230lb, intelligent dog...that was raised by wolves for the first 2 years of its life. The first time I came home from work and found him butchering a small animal in my kitchen sink with my 12" Danish steel chef's knife, I had to call Sandy over for help. In about 3 weeks we moved into a big, old house on the Hill. We worked on his civilization lessons for two months. We found out that under the naïveté, Slider had a keen intelligence lurking. He learned the rules very quickly, usually only having to be told once. Sandy would cast a glamour over him, making him look like a hugely muscled young man with a handsome face and a long red ponytail. He loved it. With this in place, we took long walks and pointed out the ways that humans interacted, and he picked it up very quickly. He was basically a predator, and this was just a new kind of camouflage for him.

Eventually we went to Gideon again, and it wasn't as hard for me this time. The singing session with Sandy had gone so well that it had become a regular thing, and he gave us an amulet that would cast the glamour over Slider as long as he wore it, and he did so nearly all the time. We renamed him Peter Avery, and soon he was a regular on Broadway, and attracting his share of admiring glances.

He broke down and cried like a baby when we told him how John had reacted to his promise gifts. It was almost the end of us, but we pulled him through it and he recovered. Eventually he started to ask if he couldn't meet John while wearing his glamour amulet. We knew it had to happen and had been dreading it for months.

Poor Slider was a mess the night we agreed to take him to the bar. He was nervous and anxious and almost backed out at the last minute, but we drug him along to the bar anyway. I could see him trembling as we walked in the door together, and he was asked for ID. He pulled out the driver's license I'd had made for him. It passed inspection and we were in.

"C'mon, Pete. The action's all upstairs, boy-o. Just follow me."

"Oh God, Ralph! What if he doesn't like me? What will I do?"

"He'll like you, Peter. You're gorgeous. This will be a cakewalk." I crossed my fingers, and hoped I wasn't lying.

John had been getting over his trauma for the last three months. He was smiling again, and handily beating just about everybody at pool just like he had before. He'd never gotten another cat, but seemed to be pretty ok. Following the incident, he and I had become sort of close friends. Now he saw us come up the stairs from the other side of the pool tables, and started over with a big smile to greet me. I felt Slider stiffen and gasp when he saw him. Yup...still head over heels. He just understood what was happening to him now, was the difference. And he knew how to act.

I enjoyed a long hug with John, then stepped back. I wanted him to notice Pete. And he did.

Ok, at 6'4" and 230lb of solid muscle, Slider is a little hard to miss. But John definitely took time to appreciate what he was noticing.

"So, who's your friend, Ralph? Don't think I've seen him around before."

"John Shea,, this is Peter Avery – but everyone calls him Pete. He's just moved to town, and he's rooming with Sandy and I."

"Nice to meet you, John. How you doin'?"

"Doin' good, Pete. Nice to meet you too. Hey, you play pool much?"

"Nah man...never did. But I always wanted to...I watch those pool tournaments on TV sometimes, y'know, and I think 'how cool is that?'"

I smiled at Sandy as John led him over to an unoccupied pool table and started teaching him the game of pool.

HEART AND HOOVES:
AN URBAN FANTASY

(1)

The first time I saw him, it was midsummer and I was working the streets up on the Hill. I was wearing my 'work clothes' – a clingy nylon tee-shirt so you could see the rings in my nips, tight jeans ripped off about midthigh, a wide, black leather, silver-spiked dog collar around my neck. I was working at projecting an air of debauched innocence (which isn't easy – try it and see). Since I was standing right outside the hardest leather bar in town, I was getting lots of looks from the leathermen walking in and out of the bar – appropriately called "The Hellhole." I was pretty sure someone was going to engage my services soon, and I'd be able to eat for a while afterward, so I was in a pretty good mood.

He wasn't much to look at: short, kinda chubby, amiable face – you know the type: the kind you could take home to Mom and Dad and expect that they'd like him. Normally not the kind I'd look at twice, 'cause I don't have much to do with nice people anymore.

The thing that caught my attention was that he set off my fey-dar like crazy. Yeah, I know all about 'gaydar,' and I got that in spades too. But it's nothing compared to how far away I can spot one of the Kin…and I usually make tracks outta there when I do. One thing I don't need is to attract the attention of some Unseelie bastard and have him make my life even more miserable just because he can. Nope, I swore off hanging with any of the fey a long time ago. I'm way over that fey pride stuff.

So this guy is strolling up the street, and I'm trying to be really inconspicuous, projecting "I'm not here" like crazy, which usually works. But when this guy draws even with me, he looks over and smiles a little and nods at me, like he's known I was there the whole time. That was when I knew he was one of the really old ones…Shit! Just my luck. I knew I'd been spotted, and it was only a matter of time before I ran into him again. I hoped I had enough smoke to survive the encounter. I knew what the old ones are like – been there, done that, barely escaped with my skin intact… most of it, anyway.

Just then one of the big dudes that had been eyeing me up and down as he went into the bar a bit ago re-emerged, and headed my way. I wiped the worry off my face – tricks don't like to see a worried look, 'cause then they think you got "issues" and that puts most of 'em right off. He leaned up against the wall next to me and lit a cigarette, not even looking at me.

"Hey boy, how much?"

"I ain't cheap man, but I play hard…and I don't use a safeword."

He took a drag on his cigarette and blew out a big cloud of blue smoke. I could see it curling in the air where the streetlight shone through it.

"I think I've heard of you, boy…been making the rounds, haven't you? Here's the deal: I get you all night, and I do whatever I want. I pay you a grand. We got a deal?"

I shrugged, acting nonchalant. "Yeah, that works. Where you want me?"

"See that black pickup over there in the pay lot? There's a big dog kennel in the back. I'm going to get another beer, and when I come out, I want to find you in that dog kennel. Naked. Got it?"

"Yeah, got it. In the dog kennel. I'll be waiting."

"Don't jerk me around, boy – I have a lot of friends in this town."

"I wouldn't, Sir. I'll be waiting for you." I hit just the right notes of nervousness and servility…sometimes I amaze myself. I won't bore you with the details of that night – let's just say that dude was tough and mean, and he liked edge-work. He'd done quite a bit of creative carving on me when he let me out of the dog kennel the next morning, right back on the Hill, and I was sporting a brand new PA that I hadn't really wanted. But at least he was honest, and I had a roll of hundreds in my pocket, and a promise that he'd tell some of his friends about me. I kissed his boots just before I drug myself off to the bus for a ride back to my place on the shore of Lake Washington. All part of the act, you know…

The bus ground to a halt at my stop, waking me out a light nap. I stumbled to the front of the bus, and the driver flashed me a concerned look.

"Hey, you ok, kid?"

"Yeah, I'm good. Just a long, hard night, dude." I gave him a weary smile, 'cause it's one of the things I love about living in Seattle – people ask if you're ok, and even mean it sometimes.

When I'm not out doing no good, I hang in this tiny little postage stamp park right on the shore of the lake. Almost nobody knows about it, and even fewer go there when the weather is anything but hot and sunny – which is most of the time. So I have the place all to myself mostly, and that suits me just fine. The folk that live in the houses adjoining the park don't pay much attention to what happens in there as long as it doesn't intrude, and I'm a pretty quiet guy, so it's no problem.

I was definitely ready for a little chill time. My back hurt hideously, and a lot of the cuts back there were still oozing, I could tell. My tee-shirt was shot to hell…better do some shopping with that K the dude gave me, too. But right then I was too tired to think about it much. I just wanted to get in the water and stop hurting.

I peeled down all the way and left my clothes lying on the bank. I walked out into the lake, feeling the weeds and mud with my toes…it felt good, like home. The cold water stung like hell in the cuts, but I ignored that, 'cause it was all gonna go away in a moment. When I was out about ten feet, and the water was up to my lower lip, I waited for just a moment, anticipating the rush of energy and the cessation of pain I knew was coming…then I took a deep breath and changed.

Thank gods the change is painless. It's quick too, which is pretty handy. One moment I'm a short, dark haired dude, and the next I'm a wicked big horse, lying low in the water. The horse is a lot meaner and trickier than when I'm a guy...the first impulse I felt after I changed was to go find that dude from last night and stomp him into road kill, but I controlled that pretty easily. I've had a lot of practice controlling those kinds of thoughts – I suppose there are a lot of people out there that deserve to be turned into a big, sticky pizza, but I don't need the trouble that sort of thing brings.

For those of you who are a little puzzled at this point, I guess I'll explain. Pay attention, cause I'm only going to tell you about this once, ok? I'm a Pooka. I didn't know that the first time I changed, and I freaked out over it, but I'm used to it now. After I changed back that first time, I looked on the Internet at the library and found out what I was...who knew? Back then, I was just a really scared kid who thought he was going to drown himself in the lake, and all of a sudden I'm this enormous, powerful horse. It was a lot to absorb.

Yeah, ok...so drowning myself didn't work out quite the way I had imagined it would. See, when I was real little, I was found wandering in a park up just north of the U-district: Cowan park, actually. DSHS found me a place to stay with a really cool couple in Leschi. I won't tell you their names, but the man was a professor at the U, and the wife ran a catering business. They were both cool as shit – had a big house next to the lake, got me into school, all the good stuff. But they had this son, Dan. How it is that two such cool people could make a mean shit like him, I'll never know. I was there about three months, doing really good and all, when he started messing with me. He told me all older guys did it to little boys, and I was naïve as hell, so what did I know? I told him to stop, but he wouldn't. When I threatened to tell the parents, he just laughed and told me to go ahead – they already knew and thought it was fine. Dude seriously fucked with my head but good. I won't go into the details, 'cause they make me antsy when I'm the horse...like I want to go out and kill something.

So after about a year, I got tired of it all, and I couldn't see any way to get out of it, so I decided to go for a really long swim in the lake, if you see what I mean. I left a little note in my mom's sock drawer, telling her goodbye and all...they were always cool to me, even if they did let their son have his way with me (which, of course, was a lie. But I didn't know that then). Then I trudged down to the dock, stripped off all my clothes, 'cause I didn't want to get 'em wet and muddy, and walked out into the lake. I ducked under and held my breath till I couldn't hold it any more...when I felt this huge surge of energy and suddenly I was standing there in the water up to my belly, and I was this enormous black horse. It was a little startling.

I didn't go back. I just spent a lot of time being the horse at first...it felt good to be strong and tricky, I'll admit. And time runs differently when I'm the horse...doesn't mean as much, I guess.

So now I'm eighteen, and I'm making my way doing what I know best. It's not much, but I'm good at it, and who cares what happens to me, anyway? I'm just street trash, for real. And if I have a little secret that nobody knows, all the better.

(2)

The next time I saw that guy, I was sitting in a booth up at Mike's, having a home cooked meal…or as close as I get to one, anyway. It was right around midnight. I was still flush from my last trick – now known as "dog kennel guy" – so I was treating myself to a real breakfast. I eat fast food a lot, so it was a pleasure to sit down to a real, honest-to-gods, eggs-bacon-and-toast meal for a change…until he walked in with a couple of his buddies.

One was a real pretty drag queen – not my type, but I can understand beauty, and she had it down to a science; the second was this huge, bodybuilder guy with long red hair – I figured the horse could take him, but as a guy, he looked like he could pull my arms and legs off without even breaking a sweat.

All three of 'em were making my feydar do back flips, but I figured if I left now, I'd be really obvious. So I decided to brazen it out and just keep eating my meal, though it was about as tasty as dead grass now – don't ask me how I know what dead grass tastes like, ok?

I saw the short dude lean over and whisper something to the pretty one, and indicate me with his eyes. I pretended to ignore the exchange and went on stuffing my face. Just as I was finishing, the short dude appeared at the corner of my booth. I

41

hadn't heard any footsteps as he approached, and my hearing is pretty good, so I was a little startled. I think I covered pretty well, though.

"Hello, my name is Ralph. May I sit?" His voice was quiet and sounded like one of those guys on public television, kinda British or something. He pronounced his name like 'Rafe,' and it wasn't till later that I found out he spelled it like the dorky kid's name.

"I'm sorry, I was just finishing up. Maybe another time... look for me outside the Hellhole, john." Yeah, I know...kinda rude, but I didn't want him to be under any illusions.

"I know you hang out there, Bryon..." His deliberate use of my name made me can the attitude real fast. "I'm not in the market for a rent boy. I just thought we could talk a little, is all."

"It's a free country, Ralph. Help yourself."

"Your time is worth something, Bryon. May I pay for your meal? No obligation beyond that, you understand."

I nodded and passed him the tab. Usually something like that would have pissed me off, but I was a little curious about this guy, against my better judgment. I mean, if the guy had gone to the trouble of finding out my name, the least I could do was let him pay for my meal, right?

He waved Everett over and handed him the ticket, telling him to add it to his tab. Everett nodded and very politely asked him if there would be anything else. He raised an inquiring eyebrow at me, but I shook my head.

"No thank you, Everett. We'll just sit and chat for a while, I think. We could have a little change of mood music-wise, though."

Everett grinned and winked just before leaving. Pretty soon, the "classic rock" that had been playing over the sound system changed to deep, dark blues – I recognized the voice of a local artist, Ernestine Anderson.

Ralph smiled. "I love that guy! Never have to tell him what I want to hear. So, Bryon...I remember seeing you outside the Hellhole the other night. What was odd was that I almost didn't see you. I've got pretty sharp eyes, you know. You're quite accomplished at hiding in plain sight."

I shrugged modestly. "It's a skill I learned awhile back. Helps with the police pretty well."

"Yes, it would have fooled a policeman entirely, I imagine. I bet you're wondering what I mean by coming over here, interrupting your meal and taking up your time like this, aren't you?"

I didn't say anything, just nodded for him to continue.

"Well, consider me the welcome wagon. You're relatively new to the neighborhood, and my two friends and I like to keep track of those who are out and about and just a bit...hmm, uncanny might be a good way of putting it."

"Thanks," I murmured. "I like it here. I might be around for awhile."

"Or you might not," he said gently. "Your profession and the particular clientele you work with does not lend itself to longevity, young Bryon. I say this not as a criticism, but only as a statement of fact, you understand."

It was an honest assessment, given that he didn't know I rejuvenated after each "session" with a little horse time. My unblemished skin would have surprised him, I think. I nodded again, to let him know I was listening, and he continued.

43

"If it would be all right with you, I'd like to ask my two friends to join us and meet you. I think you'll find them most interesting."

"Sure. Can't know too many people, right?"

"Oh yes, Bryon. One can certainly know too many people if they're not the right sort. But let me introduce you to my brothers – by adoption, if not by blood." He waved at the other two, and they made their way to the booth, one slipping in on either side of us. The big redhead sat next to me. This close, I could practically smell the fey-ness rolling off of him. This one was way, way more than he looked like. When I turned to look at the drag queen up close, I got the same sense. I winced inside – I was in very deep here. But I kept my face still and neutral, not giving a thing away.

Peter, the redhead, had hands so enormous that mine all but disappeared when he shook it. He acted shy and somehow kind of sweet, which surprised me. I should know better than to judge anyone by their looks, I guess.

The drag queen was Sandy. There was none of the affected manners that I'd seen in the few drag queens I'd ever met. This guy looked me right in the eye and his handshake was strong and masculine, even with the perfectly painted and manicured nails. We shared a few minutes of small talk, introducing ourselves and being politely social. Nothing more was said of my…err, choice of professions. The other two treated me as an equal; none of that talking down to me because I'm only eighteen that I hate so much. I relaxed a little and was just starting to enjoy myself when Ralph mentioned that they had to go. Apparently, Sandy was slated to do an after hours show at a nearby bar. After a quick glance at the other two, and a minute nod from each, Ralph extended an invitation to me.

"We'd like to meet you in a less public place, Bryon. We've decided that we like you, and we'd like to know more about you and let you know us a little more as well. Perhaps it would be convenient to come to a late supper at our home? Would this coming Friday work for you? I'm afraid it would have to be rather late. You might say that I work the night shift." He smiled a little as he said it, and Peter guffawed while Sandy only looked amused. At my nod, he continued: "Here is my card. It has my name, address and telephone number on it. Please feel free to call at any time. If none of us are around, you can leave a message, as Sandy has bullied me into getting one of those ridiculous answering services on the line." He assumed an expression of long suffering for a moment, and I couldn't help but smile a little.

Sandy smiled at his companion, but spoke to me. "It's been nice meeting you, Bryon. Please do come by for dinner on Friday. I'm sure we'll find lots to talk about."

"I'll second that, Bryon. C'mon over – Sandy is a mean cook. Put's the cooking here to shame. And mean too – he's been teaching me to cook for two months and he's still got me peeling potatoes." Peter's voice was a low rumble, and he smiled a little at Sandy.

"He can't be trusted with anything beyond a potato peeler, Bryon," Sandy interjected. "It's for his own safety. The last time he tried to use a real knife, he about cut his finger off."

All three were laughing over the incident, and I felt a momentary twinge of envy at the way they were so comfortable with each other. But I shut that down ruthlessly. I had my lot in life, and I knew it. I had to be content with what I had. But, maybe for one night I could at least see what it was like…

"I'd like that," I said, surprising myself. "How about right around nine o'clock?"

"That would do nicely, Bryon," Ralph said. "We'll look forward to it on Friday at nine, then. And now, we have to go.

Have a lovely evening, Bryon." The three of them each shook my hand again, and then walked out of the bar. I heard Sandy giving Ralph shit about acting like the lord of the manor just before they went out the door, and the two of them laughing about it. Everett came over just then and offered me an espresso of my choice, saying that it was Ralph's treat. I had a mocha grande, with three shots and raspberry. Never look a gift horse...um, well, never mind.

Wednesday, I spent the day shopping. I didn't want to show up at the trio's place looking like a refugee from a skater convention. I like that look, and when I'm not conducting business it's my usual. But I thought about how the three of them had been dressed, and realized I didn't have a thing to wear. So it was off to Nordstrom for me, to buy a killer outfit and prove that I had as much fashion sense as the next nouveau fag. I decided to pick up some shoes for the outfit as well, and a bottle of cologne that I tried on a whim and really liked. By the time I was done, I'd put a serious dent in my cash, so I knew I was going to have to turn another trick that night or the next to top it off again.

It was cloudy and windy the next night, with just a little rain mixed in; standing outside the Hellhole in what I liked to think of as my "debauched skater punk" outfit, I couldn't help shivering a little. The only constant in all my outfits is the dog collar. As I lounged against the wall, pretending to mind my own business, I didn't even hear him until he was standing right next to me. I took one look at him and knew I was in trouble.

He was a tall, slender man with coal black skin and a handsome face. He wore his leathers like a tuxedo – very elegant, very tailored and very expensive. He positively reeked of fey energy.

"I heard there was an independent working the 'hole... thought I'd come down for a little look. And lo and behold, here you are. Very accommodating, I must say. I think I might just try you out for the night. Could be entertaining, if nothing else."

"What are you talkin' about, mister? I'm just waiting for a bus," I lied, nodding at the bus stop in front of us. Ok, not a very good lie, but it was all I could think of at the moment. This guy had me seriously rattled.

The guy laughed, and it gave me the shivers. "Oh no, youngster, that won't do. You see, Jeffrey – who had the pleasure of having you a few nights agone – told me all about you. He said, and I quote 'he ain't cheap, but he plays hard…and he doesn't use safewords.' Does that sound familiar?"

Ah, shit. I knew I was going to regret saying that one of these days. But I decided to brazen it out.

"Naw, man. Never heard anything like that before. You got the wrong dude."

"I don't think so, little man," he replied "or should I say little pooka? I know all about you. It's been a very long time since I played with one of your kind, and I'm inclined to try you. So, be a good little boy and come with me." He snapped his fingers in front of my eyes, and I felt my body go strangely distant, like I'd been shoved out of my own skull. When he started to walk away, I found myself walking behind him at three paces distance, whether I wanted to or not. I struggled to regain my body, but it was useless. I was along for the ride and that was all there was to it.

We walked about two blocks and turned onto a side street, and there was a huge BMW sedan waiting at the curb. At our approach, a man slid out of the driver's seat, walked around and opened the rear door. My captor slid in and I followed him, sitting on the elegant leather upholstery. Dimly, I could feel it, cool against my back through my thin shirt. The driver shut the door, locking me into the nightmare. I was still struggling with the mind lock this bastard had on me, but it was more reflexive than anything – I knew he had me.

We drove out to a big place in Laurelhurst. It was surrounded by high stone walls, and a heavy iron gate slid aside as the car purred up the drive. Not that unusual in this neighborhood, I was guessing. Strangely, I wasn't feeling a lot of fear. That changed when I looked at my host, though. Once through the gate, he dropped his glamour. I recognized him for what he was immediately – the tall, sharply pointed ears, dark complexion and narrow, uptilted eyes were a dead giveaway. He was a Drow, a dark elf. If I'd thought I was in trouble before, now I knew it.

When we entered the house, I heard the lock click behind me. I knew that lock was the least of my worries. That door was probably warded 'til Tuesday, and there was no way anyone was going in or out of that door till my captor wanted them to. No, the lock was for my benefit: the first round in the effort to break me down. I have to admit, it worked a little.

I stood there docilely as two enormous things shambled out of the shadows in the front hall and each took one of my arms in huge hands. They looked like someone had modeled titans in plastic and then hit them with a blowtorch – sort of melted and amorphous. There was nothing wrong with their grip, though. There was no way I was going anywhere. The Drow snapped his fingers in front of my face again, and I was back in my own mind, back in control, if you want to call it that. I was suddenly so afraid I nearly peed my pants. I struggled against the hands holding my arms, but it was useless. They were way too strong.

"Hmm, I like that, boy. Struggle some more, won't you? Maybe you could scream a little too," the Drow mocked me. Behind him, another dark elf walked out of a side door. "Arturo, take this young man downstairs to the playroom, would you? I think he's going to make a lovely evening's entertainment."

The second drow bowed, then snapped his fingers at whatever the things holding my arms were, and they dragged me along behind his retreating back, further into the house.

In the basement, there was…well, there's no easy way to put this: there was a torture chamber. It looked more like a surgery unit: all white, with big overhead lights and a table in the middle with movable parts, drapes laid over everything so neatly. But the instruments laid out on the side table didn't look like anything I'd seen on ER, believe me. Nor do most surgical units have electric branding irons included.

Finally, the drow who brought me to the basement spoke, but not to me. He was thinking out loud:

"M'lord Braewynn insists on bringing home the dirtiest specimens, I swear. Where on earth does he find them? This one looks like he's been rolling with pigs. Well, nothing for it but a bit of a wash." With that, he turned and started for a door on the side of the room, waving my walking restraints along behind him.

My heart began to pound in my chest, but I kept the look of abject fear on my face. The room we entered was tiled all in white. There was an enormous, rectangular tub filled with water in the center of the room. Braewynn's toady was about to make a serious mistake, but I didn't say a word. The two dudes holding me lifted me up and plunged me face first into the freezing water in the tub.

The second the water closed over me, the change swept over my body like a tornado. No need to will it to come this time – the horse was desperate to come out and play. I lunged up out of that tub like a drow's worst nightmare, and I had every intention of playing the part. I shook off the things holding me like rats, spun and kicked one into the far wall with a sickening thud. The other came at me again, and I bit it and shook it like a terrier.

Arturo tried the mind lock trick again, but the horse shrugged it off like so much rotten cheesecloth. I charged him, shouldered him out of the way and kicked him with a hind leg as I went by. Above me, I dimly heard Braewynn bellowing something about what a fool Arturo was, but that was none of my concern. I wanted out of there, and right now wasn't soon enough.

One good kick was enough to account for the door at the top of the stairs leading up to the first floor, and I flowed out of the door and into the hall there like a dervish, hooves clattering and skidding on the marble floor. I knew I couldn't get out the front door, but I was hoping there was a back door, so I turned left and headed deeper into the house.

That was when I met Braewynn. He was standing about ten feet away. He didn't even try for pacifying measures: the moment he saw me, he cut loose with a levin bolt that would have fried me if it had hit, but I smoothly dodged it and was on him before he could whip up another. I hit him full on, and drove right on over him. I'd have liked to have paused and danced on him a little, but by now an alarm was screaming throughout the whole house and I could hear heavy footsteps coming down the stairs behind me. So, as much as the horse wanted to finish the job, I sprinted forward and smashed another door to find myself in a library, with tall windows overlooking a garden.

Two strides took me across the room, and I leaped like a hunter, right through those windows. They were warded as well, but mostly to keep things outside from getting in so I just got the tiniest effect, and I only got a little singed. In the garden, I spun back to the house and reared high on my hindquarters, screaming defiance, raking the air with my forelegs. Braewynn appeared at the broken window of the library, looking worse for the wear, and threw another levin bolt, but this one was a lot weaker and I dodged it easily. Then I spun around and galloped the length of the garden, gathering speed and power. When I reached the wall, I rose over it like a bird, and landed lightly on the other side. Without a glance back I hit the road, accelerating to a full, wild gallop within three strides and disappeared into the night, with only the triple beat of a racing stride to mark my passage.

(3)

A couple years earlier, I had discovered an abandoned garage that everyone seemed to have forgotten, and it had become my bolt hole. It was far enough away from the park to not be associated with my presence there, but close enough to reach in an emergency. So, I vanished into my little refuge for the remainder of the night. I spent a lot of time thinking about my situation...which pretty much sucked no matter how I looked at it. Drows are the masters of Unseelie, and the Unseelie Court operates on strength and pride. Looking back on the earlier events, I realized I should have finished the job like the horse had wanted to do, 'cause there was no way Braewynn could let this go now. His position in court was dependent on him looking strong, and getting trashed in your own home by an eighteen year old boy does not foster an image of strength. So he was going to be gunning for me, needing to reassert himself. Essentially, my ass was in a sling.

What I needed were allies, someone who would watch my back. I was strong enough to take on most of the baddies one-on-one, but I was no good in a firefight, and I knew that was what this was going to devolve into.

Damn...I didn't know anybody who'd be willing to put it on the line for me. I'd never made any friends, and I knew damn well none of my tricks were going to help me, even if they could.

That was when I remembered Ralph and his posse. There was a big ol' downside to asking them, 'cause it would mean I'd be indebted to them forever, or pretty damn close to... but what choice did I have? I didn't have enough smoke to try and take on Braewynn and his whole crowd by myself, and while I didn't know exactly what their trip was, it was more than obvious to me that the three of them were heavy hitters. Still, they'd treated me pretty well at Mike's, so there was at least a chance I could come out of this ok. Better get it over with, I supposed; a chance was better than nothing.

When sunlight started to filter in through the small, grimy windows, I checked around pretty carefully to make sure no one was watching, then I changed into the most nondescript clothes I had, packed my new clothes into a shopping bag and slid out of a broken window in the garage. I hopped a bus going downtown, and then another that would take me to Southcenter Mall, way south of town. I'd been there a time or two before, and been surprised by how many of the fey hung out at the mall. I figured that since Braewynn wouldn't be advertising what happened last night, no one would know to report that I was hanging out down there, and being around all those other fey might throw his hunters off the track a little.

There was only one real problem with my plan: I hate malls. I know, I can't be a member of my generation in good standing if I don't love malls and all that, but they're just so bloodless, so completely without life. Cardboard, plastic and bullshit is about all they're made of, and I hate phony. Give me the little old downtowns of some of the outlying burghs like Burien any day. They have a sense of history, a life that appeals to me. The mall? Nada. But, desperate times call for desperate measures, so I sucked it up and spent most of the day there. Finally, around three pm or so, I couldn't stand it anymore and took a bus back to Broadway.

I stopped in at a Starbucks and used their bathroom, where I pulled on my new outfit – they'd suddenly gone from being party clothes to 'begging for help' clothes – spritzed with the cologne, and was ready to walk over to Ralph's place. I'd memorized the print on the card after Ralph gave it to me and then I'd destroyed it, so I walked over to the address, skulking along the back streets and trying to watch my back as best I could. I didn't see anything that obviously meant I'd been spotted, but if Braewynn was any good at all, I wouldn't have. Is it still paranoia if you know someone is out to get you? Yet another question to ponder in my spare time, I suppose.

The address turned out to be an enormous old Victorian up by Volunteer Park. It was beautifully restored, but not painted in the usual pastels – this one was dark forest green with deep mulberry trim. I admired the house for a moment from the street, then walked up the stairs to the gate. It was cold iron, so I hopped over it, being careful not to touch it. Thank gods most things are made of stainless steel these days – iron burns like a motherfucker. I noted that directly behind the tall hedge of Arbor Vitae that surrounded the house was a high fence of black wrought iron. It seemed to crackle with energy to my sight, and it gave me hope that these guys weren't clueless.

So, up onto the porch I went. The front door had a big lion's head knocker, and I politely tapped the bar on the plate and waited for someone to answer. I heard footsteps approach the door, and then Peter opened it.

"Well, this is a surprise. You're a little early," he said, smiling. "I'm afraid Sandy hasn't started dinner yet."

"Hi Peter, is Ralph around? I was wondering if I could talk to him for a little while."

"He's still sleeping, kid. Say, you look kinda nervous…you wanna come in?"

"I'd be grateful if I could, Peter."

"Then, c'mon in. He won't be up for a while, I'm thinkin'."

As I walked through the door, my whole skin tingled as the wards let me through. Good thing I wasn't trying to get in without permission: there was some heavy-duty magic on that door. It gave me more hope, actually.

The house was full of old furniture, as beautifully restored as the outside of the house. The windows were mullioned, with lots of beveled glass that would cast spectrums all over the rooms when the sun was out. All neat as a pin inside too, which I liked. I hate clutter.

Peter led me into a small parlor and waved me to an overstuffed sofa. "I'll go get Sandy. Maybe he can help. Wait here." Then he turned and walked out, and I could the floor creaking a little as he walked away.

Sitting in that parlor and cooling my heels was one of the hardest things I'd ever done. I wanted to get up and pace, and the horse was anxious inside me, urging me to find water and let him out. I thought quieting thoughts at him, and managed to chill him out a little. The horse and I get along pretty good, and it's because we respect each other. I suppose I could stuff him down and put a cap on it if I really wanted to, but we're brothers and allies, the horse and I.

"Peter, are you in…Oh! Hello. Didn't expect to see you in here."

"Oh yeah, well, um...I decided to come over a little early. I hope it's ok?"

"It's not a problem...you're welcome, of course. I haven't started dinner, but if you don't mind the wait..."

"Yeah... um, about that. It might not be a bad idea to sort of... reschedule that. Something came up that I sort of wanted to talk to Ralph about."

"Ah. Well, I think he'll be here, but it might be a bit of a wait. Is there something I could help with?"

"Um...well, let me run the situation by Ralph first, ok? It isn't that I don't trust you or anything..."

"I understand, Bryon. Ralph is pretty easy to talk to, isn't he? Since we're postponing dinner, can I get you something to eat? It might be a bit of a wait before Ralph is ready to come down."

I tried to keep a hungry look off of my face, but I think Sandy saw right through it because he just laughed, waved me along behind him, and led me to the kitchen. He installed me on a stool at a breakfast bar and then started pulling stuff out of the 'fridge, some of which I didn't even know what it was. He loaded up a plate and zapped it hot in the microwave, and then set it in front of me with a knife and fork. I was a little embarrassed by the way I dug in, but I hadn't eaten since the day before. He just smiled, poured himself a glass of wine and sat across the counter from me, watching me eat and making small talk.

Gods, the guy was funny as hell. Some of the stuff he was saying had me rollin', I swear. He had this skewed sense of humor that had me thinking and laughing at the same time. I hadn't had this much fun without a beer or a bong in a long time. When I finished what was on the plate, Sandy put it with the silverware in the sink and led me down a little hall, through a pair of narrow french doors and back into the parlor, all the while both of us chatting like old friends. I almost forgot why I'd come there in the first place. I didn't realize how fast the time was going until Peter stepped into the room and said that Ralph was awake, and would be down in a minute.

"Well Bryon, it's been a pleasure. I'll let you talk with Ralph now, and maybe we can talk again later. You won't forget to reschedule dinner, right?" I nodded, but I couldn't seem to dredge up a smile. The whole messy reality of the last couple days had hit me again.

As he stood and walked out of the room, Ralph passed him at the door. His hair was slicked back today, not in it's usual Beethoven-ish mess. Sandy flicked a smile at him and then headed off back toward the kitchen. Ralph paused and shut the open side of the French doors, then turned and sat himself on the same wing-back chair that Sandy had recently vacated. I hoped he couldn't see my anxiety.

"Um, thanks for seeing me, Ralph. Um…I got a little problem, see…and…"

Ralph smiled warmly at me, and I felt myself start to relax a little. "Relax, Bryon. You're among friends here, or I hope you will be, in any case. Why don't you tell me what's happened, starting at the top. Nice outfit, by the way."

I smiled a little, distracted for a moment by his compliment, just as he intended me to be, I suspected. "Yeah, I had a few bucks and decided to do a little shopping."

"Clothes make the man, Bryon. Good choice. Now, why don't you tell me what's happened, right from the start?"

"Well, remember what you said the other night about knowing too many people if they were the wrong sort?"

He nodded but didn't speak.

"Well, that sort of happened..." And I proceeded to spill out the whole sorry tale. He didn't interrupt even once, just listened intently, leaning forward a little and looking right at me. I saw his face tighten briefly the first time I mentioned Braewynn's name, but then he listened just the same as before.

"So I beat feet for the lakeshore and swam home, then holed up all day till I came over here," I finished up, streamlining events a little.

"Well, that's quite a tale, Bryon. Let me think for a moment." He sat back in the chair and closed his eyes. He stayed that way for about three minutes, and it seemed like eternity to me.

Finally, he opened his eyes and looked at me. "There are several things we're going to need to discuss, lad. Let me say first that you handled the situation extremely well. Had you allowed the horse to stomp Braewynn to death, you would be in infinitely greater danger than you are at present. Braewynn is placed very highly in Unseelie Court, and since he did not intend to kill you, his death would have been considered unwarranted. You'd have been declared a murderer, and a price put on your head, at which time any Fey with a desire for gold could – and would – have been trying to kill you. So avoiding that was a stroke of luck for you."

"But...but he wanted to torture me! Doesn't that count?"

"Not torture you, Bryon...break your will and make you submit to him. Yes, the difference seems unimportant to us, but in the eyes of the Unseelie, it's everything. He wouldn't have killed you because, whether you know it or not, you are an extremely

58

valuable commodity to him." He must have seen the startled and bewildered look on my face, because he laughed softly before continuing.

"What do you know about the War of the Courts, Bryon?"

"War of the Courts? Um…well, nothing actually…"

Ralph sighed. "I thought as much. What do they teach children in school these days?" He smiled again at me, and I smiled back a little to show I knew he was playing with me. Then his look got very serious again. "Listen well then, Bryon. I may only get to tell you this once, and it's of gravest consequence."

"A thousand years ago, give or take a decade or two, Seelie and Unseelie went to war. I hear that it was because a young prince of Unseelie Court offered insult to a princess of Seelie, but everyone I talk to gets very vague when I ask about it. It doesn't really matter why, I suppose. What matters is that it happened. Harsh and irretrievable words were spoken by both sides, and suddenly no one could honorably withdraw. They chose the American continent for their battlefield, since there weren't any europeans there at the time. The local powers warned the native americans who lived here to withdraw, and that left the field open for the fey.

"Picture it, Bryon: Every monster and magical being of myth and legend that was ever known, and many that weren't, lined up in great battle formations, readying for the attack. Proud banners and pennants snapping in the breeze, the sun glinting on polished armor and arms. Perhaps Unseelie held a slight advantage in numbers, but it was met and matched by the power of Seelie martial prowess and discipline…it must have been a brave sight indeed. I daresay, the angels in heaven themselves stopped and looked down to witness the sight.

"And here, Bryon, is where you and your ancestors come in. The lords and ladies (oh yes, the ladies of the courts did not shun battle, you may be sure) of Seelie Court all rode *Raithen*, what we call elvensteeds today. But no elvensteed would ever allow aught of Unseelie to ride them, so the lords and ladies of Unseelie rode pookas into battle, whether the pookas wished it or no. They were aligned with Unseelie, and must obey their lieges, you see. While not as fast as the elvensteeds, they were far superior in intelligence, and ferocious warriors in their own right.

"So, at the appointed hour, the silvery clarions of Seelie rang out, echoed by powerful blasts from the deep voiced battle horns of Unseelie, and the two great armies moved out, crossing the mile of open land between them in a heartbeat and each smashing headlong into the line of the opposing army. The crash of that meeting shook the continent.

"It was a disaster. The armies were too evenly matched for one to prevail over the other. The battle magics of each side essentially cancelled each other out, and while Unseelie had fielded a slightly larger army, Seelie had the vantage in discipline and skill of arms. And so they remained locked in pitiless battle for three days and two nights. Great was the slaughter as a million petty insults and quarrels were redressed. Finally, as the sun set on the third day, the two kings met on the battlefield. But as their retinues of fell warriors approached one another, a great and terrible thing happened.

"Suddenly, out of thin air, the queens of both courts appeared between the approaching lines: of Unseelie, Maeve – more beautiful than the starriest new moon night, and of Seelie, Gloriana – glorious as the brightest, sun-drenched day. Each held a dagger to the throat of the other.

"In one voice, so powerful that every being on the entire battlefield heard each word they spoke, they cried "Hold, great kings! For love of your queens and your peoples, hold! Whosoever should slay another, that court's queen shall die, followed by her sister queen, who shall slay herself for shame."

Then Gloriana spoke, and the power of her voice rolled across the battlefield. "Great Alberich, two sons and a daughter have I lost on this field in the heat of battle. I say, no more!"

Then Maeve also spoke. "Owen, my king and my husband, our only son has been sacrificed on the altar of hatred and wounded dignity. I, too, say it: no more!" All the while, each held a dagger in white knuckled hand to the throat of the other.

Both Kings paused, recognizing the mortal danger to their well loved wives, and looked about them. Full two thirds of the armies they each had fielded lay dead upon the plain, heaped up in windrows of death, and picked at by a great multitude of carrion crows and vultures. Everywhere they looked, they saw the shattered bodies of their kindred, and the sight smote their hearts. As one, they doffed their helms, dismounted, and approached their queens and wives where they stood, daggers still in hand.

"Be at peace, great queens both, and mothers of your people. No more blood shall Seelie shed this day." Alberich's voice was gentle, his reason finally restored.

"Your word upon it, Alberich," snapped Maeve, her dark eyes hard and bright as obsidian. "No less shall abate your wife's mortal danger."

"Likewise, Owen! Nothing less than a binding oath from each will place your wife's wellbeing in your hands." Gloriana's face was pale and hard as she glared at the king of Unseelie.

"The two kings looked at each other and shrugged helplessly, knowing they had been outmaneuvered. And so, great and binding oaths were sworn by all who remained upon the field and the daggers were withdrawn at last from the throats of the gallant ladies. For three days after were the bodies of the slain burned there on the field, and the hurts of the wounded healed. Neither Queen rested nor left the field till the last of the dead were burned and buried, and the smallest hurt bound up. And so ended the War of the Courts."

"Whoa...that's amazing. So...what's this got to do with me?"

"Many kinds of the Kin were devastated in the war. All the dryads for the elm trees, for instance, were killed. While it wasn't quite as bad for your kind, it was bad enough – a mere handful survived, and of those many more died from wounds that were seemingly minor and should have healed, but their spirits were wounded, you see. Given that, they were released from their vassalage and declared themselves neutral, aligned to neither side. They withdrew, and very little has been seen of them since. And forever after, Seelie and Unseelie have held to an elaborate system of dueling to resolve conflicts, allowing for the avoidance of mass bloodshed."

"So...you said I was a valuable commodity to Braewynn? I'm not sure I see it."

"The lords and ladies of Unseelie have missed their mounts, Bryon. They want them back. If Braewynn could break you and force an oath of allegiance from you, it would give Unseelie a toehold on the neutrality of the rest of your people – a place to start reasserting their claim, so to speak."

"So could I challenge Braewynn to a duel over this? I mean, I could see being kidnapped, held against my will and threatened with torture being an insult."

"Unfortunately, no. You're nonaligned, and that means you have no standing for a challenge."

"Hmm…ok." I sat for a moment and thought, getting more depressed by the minute. "Ok, Ralph, thanks for the information. I guess I'd better get going. Thanks for having me over."

"You don't want our help? I thought that was why you came over here, Bryon."

"Well…yeah…it would be helpful and all…but, I don't want to drag you guys into my problems."

"I think it would be helpful if Peter and Sandy joined us, and we talked this over, don't you? There may be options you haven't considered."

Reluctantly, I sat back on the sofa as he rose from the wing-back chair and headed out into the house. I heard a door open somewhere on the same floor, and Ralph's voice, speaking too quietly for me to tell what he was saying.

Just then, Peter sauntered into the room. "Hey, where's Ralph? You guys done talking?"

"Naw," I said. "He's out there somewhere talking to Sandy. You might as well stay…he wanted all three of us to talk for a little while."

"Oh, I see. All right, then…mind if I sit next to you?" Without waiting for an answer, he crashed down next to me on the sofa, which creaked alarmingly. "Damn, gotta remember to go easy on all this old furniture. I don't know why Ralph and Sandy insist on buying all this old, used stuff when they could get brand new furniture. And it's not like they even pay less for this old stuff."

I grinned at him. "Well, I don't know exactly, but I guess they call the old stuff antiques, and…"

Just then, Ralph came back into the room, trailed by Sandy, who'd changed out of the khakis and button-down he'd been wearing earlier and was wearing a pair of sweats and a muscle shirt. I shook my head a little – damn! He was just as beautiful as a boy as he was as a girl. Some people have all the luck.

After sitting back down in the wing-back chair, with Sandy sinking onto a big hassock next to him, Ralph looked at me, and then at the other two.

"I think it's time for Bryon to learn what we really are. He's got a problem that he's going to need a little help with, and he needs to know that we can help him, I think."

The other two nodded. The change in Sandy was instantaneous – one moment he was sitting there on the big foot stool, looking like a very hot guy, but definitely human. The next, his humanity melted away and I realized he was a lios alfar, a light elf…the kind that ruled Seelie court as the Drow did Unseelie. Fuck…this was getting weirder by the moment.

But that was not the end of the surprises, because next to me, Peter reached into the neck of his shirt and fished out a gold necklace with a big, red, stone pendant, and lifted it over his head; suddenly he changed, too…still enormous, but suddenly much less human. His mouth was huge and filled with big, triangular teeth that looked like a shark's and he had a red, knit hat on his head…he was a redcap. Finally, almost numb with astonishment, I looked over at Ralph and he'd changed as well – his eyes burned red, and long sharp fangs stuck down from his upper jaw, the tips just visible against his lower lip. His skin was dead white and seemed to glow just a little.

"Umm, ok…I'd love to show my true colors too, but I'd have to borrow a bathtub to do it," I stammered. "I guess you'll have to take my word for it – I'm a pooka."

"Wow," said Sandy, "that's amazing. Been a long time since one of you guys have been around. Not since the war, as I recall."

"Indeed, Sandy... and that's what lies at the heart of Bryon's problem."

"Oh? Maybe we should hear more about this. Why don't you fill us in, Bryon?"

So I told the whole sorry tale again, keeping it simple and to the point. I wasn't looking for sympathy from these guys, after all.

Ok, I was, but I didn't want to sound like I was.

"Hmm... convergence of interests, eh Ralph?" Sandy looked seriously at his friend.

"Oh yeah. I was thinking the same thing as he was telling me about his encounter with the pimp."

"The pimp? You mean Braewynn? I guess that shouldn't surprise me... but why are you guys interested in him?"

Peter spoke up then, and there was a hard edge to his deep, gravelly voice. "He's been doin' things we don't like. He steals little kids and sells 'em to whoever can pay his prices. Makes movies and stuff of 'em, too. It's not right, Bryon!"

"Well put, Slider." There was a dangerous quietness to Sandy's voice. I remembered how much the light elves loved children, then. I'd heard it was because they had so few of their own. "We'd love to put that bastard out of business."

"And it's our intention to do so… but we have to have enough evidence, and he's a sly one. The rules of court don't allow for a challenge over anything that involves only humans. We were going to go to Seelie court with a complaint when we had solid evidence against him, and hope to initiate action against him that way. But…" Ralph's voice faded on the word, and Sandy cut in.

"But now we may not have to. We can solve our problem and yours too, with one action. But you're going to have to be willing to work with us on this, Bryon." Sandy still looked calm and composed, but I could hear the excitement behind the façade.

"Um…'work with you'? What would that involve, exactly?"

"Well, I think you'd need to stay here for a couple of days while we pull something together. If Braewynn got a hold of you again, it'd be bad."

I sighed. I knew what that meant. When would I realize that good things don't last? "Okay," I said wearily. "Which one of you do I have to sleep with to get your help? Or is it all of you?"

There was a moment of stunned silence. I looked around, and they were all looking at me like I'd sprouted a third head.

"What? You think I don't know the score? Help doesn't come for free, does it? I'm an adult, and I pay with what I got."

"Oh, Bryon…" Sandy murmured.

"Three of us in this room are adults," Ralph said sharply, "though Slider is still rather young. You, on the other hand, are not an adult. The help we offer is entirely free. If you don't wish to accept our help, you are free to refuse it and there will be no retaliation. If you choose to accept it, there will be no strings attached to it, nor will there be any talk of 'repayment'. Is that clear, young man?"

"Hey!" I flared. "Don't talk to me like I'm a kid, got it? I know how it works. Nothing is for free. You say 'no strings'? I say, bullshit: everything's got strings – some are just longer than others."

"Don't be talkin' to Ralph like that, Bryon. I don't like it much," rumbled Slider.

"Wait, Slider. Ralph, calm down," Sandy cut in. "He's right, you know. He deserves to know our terms, even if he put it a little crudely." Turning to me, he continued, "Here's what we're talking about, Bryon. We are offering you haven and hospitality until this matter is resolved. This means you will be our houseguest, if you choose to be. We feed you, give you a place to sleep and, if necessary, clothe you. We keep you safe. You are involved in the planning process of any actions we take. In return, you share your information about our enemy, and agree to at least consider cooperating with our plans. We, none of us, may touch you in a sexual way while you dwell under this agreement, even should you wish us to. All this on our honors."

"On your honor? What, like the boy scouts? That's whack!" I glared at Sandy, who was suddenly looking shocked.

"I will make allowance for you, boy, because you don't know, and because you have been among humans too long. Honor, for one such as I, is not an easy concept that is put on and taken off like a pair of underwear, as it is among humans. Honor is what I am. I would die or kill to defend the verity of my honor. Do not forget this!" Deep anger burned in the green eyes he turned on me.

"Ok, ok, dude! Chill out. I didn't know. And I accept your offer. Am I allowed to leave the house?"

"The house is heavily protected, and will withstand anything short of an all out assault by our enemies. It is the safest place for you right now. Should you leave it, we'll try to keep you safe, but it will be a lot harder. Still, we can't stop you if you really want to leave."

"Ok. I get it. Stay in the house if I want to be safe."

"I think that's enough for tonight," Ralph said. "Bryon has agreed to be our ally in this problem. There's a comfortable bed in the guest room where you can sleep, Bryon. Why don't you try to get some rest? We'll talk more about this tomorrow."

The big clock out in the hall had chimed one am a few minutes before, and I was worn out. I nodded, and yawned hugely.

"Slider, perhaps you could show Bryon to his room?" Ralph's voice was warm and friendly, letting me know the conversation of a moment ago was not a problem.

Sandy rose and stepped up to me, but carefully did not touch me. "It's good to have you with us, Bryon. I think we'll lick this problem."

"Good as done, man!" I smiled at the pale elf. "Who's gonna stand a chance against four such chill dudes as us?" I turned and followed Peter, hoping I was fooling someone with my bravado. It wasn't working for me, in any case.

(4)

I awoke the next morning in a strange room. When my eyes opened, instead of open sky and birds singing, there was silence, and a white plaster ceiling, elaborately moulded with a geometric leaf pattern. I felt like I was lying on a cloud, and the voluminous white bed linens reinforced the feeling.

From my place on the bed, I glanced around the room. There were two leaded glass windows letting in the morning sunlight. They seemed to have an odd, random design of glass shards with a strange pattern of lead connecting them. I tried to make sense of the pattern, but there didn't seem to be any. It seemed to compel my attention, and I found myself getting out of bed to walk over to the closest window and look at it more closely. As I was reaching out to touch the smooth glass, there was a knock at the bedroom door.

"Come in," I yelled, my attention still focused on the window. I heard the door open as I was reaching out to trace the patternlessness of the glass.

"Don't touch that!" Sandy's voice rang across the room, and a moment later I felt his grip on my arm, pulling me back. The distraction seemed to break the fascination I'd felt for the window, and I shook my head, bewildered.

"The windows are warded, Brian. Watch this." Sandy took a pencil out of the breast pocket of his shirt, and with a single smooth, overhand gesture, threw the pencil at the window. When the point struck the glass, there was a crackle of energy and the pencil rebounded violently, whistling across the room to bury itself point first in the wall opposite. Sandy smiled thinly and pulled the pencil out of the plaster.

"Breakfast is ready, and I don't know how long Peter is going to wait for us," he said. I nodded, pulled on a pair of socks and, still wearing the sweats they'd given me to sleep in, followed him out of the room.

Downstairs, breakfast was as good as I'd hoped it would be. Peter had been right – no disloyalty to Mike's, of course – but the crisp bacon, basted eggs and perfect toast were in a different class. I had all of that and a bowl of oatmeal with raisins and brown sugar. I heard the horse practically moaning inside my head. Gotta do nice things for my buddy once in awhile, you know.

Over breakfast, Sandy filled me in on how the day would go. He had some errands to run this morning, and would be gone for several hours. Ralph was upstairs asleep, of course. Slider would be home, but was going to be busy working on his homework – he was working on earning his GED, apparently. I shot him a surprised look and he scowled and nodded.

"Sandy's idea," he commented. "Says I can't be an uneducated dolt all my life. I told him I'd done all right up to this point, but he wasn't buying it."

"What you won't do for a brother, eh?" I said.

"That's the truth of it, Bryon. I owe these guys my life, you know. I'd do anything for them."

I nodded, not knowing what the hell he was talking about, but I made a note to myself to ask more about that later. So they took off to do whatever they were going to do, and I found myself at loose ends. I read a magazine for a little while, but it was all just political crap, and I got bored pretty fast. So I decided to do a little exploring in the house. I figured it made sense to start at the bottom of the house and work my way up, so I took myself off to the basement to get started.

I found the stairs to the basement behind a small door off the kitchen. I'd sort of thought the basement would be all cement floors and exposed beams holding up the floor above, but I should have known better. The floor of the room I stepped into was hardwood, with really big Persian looking rugs laid over it. The walls had dark wood panels up to about waist height, and a chair rail above that, and a dark faux finish of several shades of red on up to the silver-gray ceiling. I know...sounds strange doesn't it? But it worked. I was a little envious of the person who came up with that idea.

There were two big rooms down there, with a wall that cut the basement in half. One seemed to be for storage and laundry, with a small half-bath, and the other was larger with a huge TV and a state-of-the-art sound system. There was a CD collection in a rack next to the sound system, and I read the titles: Mahler, Bach, Dvorak, Chopin, Debussy...not a Korn album to be seen. Damn!

I left the music undisturbed and walked over to the piano that stood against one wall across the room from the TV. I let my fingers plunk down on a couple of keys, then moved on. The front of the piano said Bosendorfer...I'd never heard of it.

I wandered into the second room: work bench against one wall, laundry machines against the back wall, half-bath in the middle. Nothing terribly interesting...until I walked past the bathroom. From the opposite wall, the one that divided the basement into two rooms, I felt a tingle. What the hell was that? Felt like wards of some kind, but pretty weak. What would need to be warded down here? I walked over to the wall, and about two feet from it, felt the all-over tingle that happens when you walk through a warding that is letting you in.

On the other side of the ward, the wall looked considerably different than it did from outside the ward...it had a built in glamour to fool the eye. Set into the wall was a beautiful door, arched across the top and hung on elaborately wrought silver hinges, with a large silver knob that gleamed like the moon in the low light of the basement. I was fascinated. I thought for a moment about the fact that I hadn't been invited to just barge in wherever I wanted, but then I remembered – "haven and hospitality." Surely that covered opening strange doors in my host's basement. And I was pretty sure it just opened into the other room anyway, though I hadn't noticed the door from the other side when I was in the other room.

So I reached out and grasped the doorknob and turned it, pulling it to me. The door swung out noiselessly, and immediately I smelled a light floral aroma, and the scent of wet grass.

Nothing could have prepared me for what was on the other side of that door. When I first looked in, I literally couldn't breathe for a moment.

It was a garden...how inadequate the word is to describe what I saw. A full moon rode high over the grounds, drenching the entire scene in silvery light. The evening star, beloved by the lios alfar, shone gently in the opposite quarter of the night sky. In front of me, a shining white peacock strutted and shimmered its feathers, letting out its haunting cry. Further away, across a wide sward, near the edge of a wood, white deer with golden antlers dipped their heads and fed on the verdant grass. A small lake, its surface littered with lilies, lay to my left. In front of me stood a small and delicately arching gazebo, with two opposing couches taking up much of its floor space. I smelled jasmine and night blooming gentians on the slight breeze. It was altogether enchanting, and I stood in awe for long moments and just let my eyes soak in the wonder of this totally unexpected gift. For the first time in a long time, I felt a sense of peace steal over me, overcoming my worries and doubts about all the problems that existed on the other side of the door I'd come through.

I walked hesitantly over to the gazebo and sat down on one of the sofas, a strange sense of lassitude coming over me. I felt every hour of the stress and worry of the last week pressing down on me, and I suddenly could hardly keep my head up or my eyes open. Standing, I wandered toward the lily pond and stood awhile, watching koi the size of my arm rise to the surface and dip back down, leaving rings of slowly expanding ripples behind them. It was as I was standing there, watching the rings of ripples disperse and reappear, that I saw movement on the lawn out of the corner of my eye, and slowly turned my head.

A tall, cloaked figure was striding toward me, across the grass. Undisturbed, the deer continued to graze as it passed by them, moving aside minutely and then dropping their heads to graze again. I knew I should be alarmed at being approached by this stranger, but I couldn't seem to muster up the energy to feel anything in particular except an abstracted kind of curiosity.

The stranger strode up to me, and stopped about five feet away. I couldn't make out any features under the drape of the figure's enveloping cloak, so I simply stood silently and waited to see what would happen.

For a long moment, the stranger stood motionless and simply looked at me. Finally, two finely boned and pale hands emerged from within the depths of the almost robe-like cloak, rose to the hood and cast it back. An elven woman stood before me, and if my feydar had been doing backflips when I met Ralph and his brothers, now it was doing a full floor routine. Even through the somnolence of the garden, I felt a tingle of power run through me. She seemed to radiate potency, and I knew if she'd meant me harm, I'd already be dead. I kept quiet and tried to look unruffled.

"For one hunted by such as Braewynn you take very rash chances, young pooka. Still, it is a delight to my eye to see one of your kind after the long years. Your tribe has been missed among the Kin."

"Lady," I said – it seemed her rightful title – "who are you? Have you known other pookas, then?"

"You are as abrupt as a human, boy. Shall I school you in manners? Very well…a gentleman would show me to a seat on yon couches, to start." Her words, while severe, carried such a tone of light amusement that I smiled and offered my arm. She delicately laid one pale hand on it and I led her to the gazebo, settled her on one of the couches, then stood awkwardly in front of her, not knowing what to do next. She gracefully gestured to a spot next to her, and I sat down.

"While it is not my name, you may call me Elenore. It has no power of calling over me, but perchance should I hear it called on the breeze by one such as you, I might be moved to respond, young sir. Thrice only may you use it."

Even someone as unschooled as I was recognized that for the gift it was. I bowed my head, and thanked her humbly.

"Attend, young pooka, for we have many things to discuss. Our time is short, for Braewynn feels your presence in the midlands even now."

"The midlands?" I asked. "What's that?"

"This garden is located not in your world, but in the lands between your world and the worlds of the elder folk. There is much magic here, and your presence in this place creates a ripple, much like the koi in the bourne, yonder. If the one who seeks you is alert, and I assure that your foe is indeed so, he will detect your presence here by that ripple. Therefore, we must speak in haste, though it pains me to do so. This is a place for long conversation, is it not? My son has brought a small piece of faerie to him, since he feels he can dwell no longer in our larger domain."

"Your son, Lady? Who are you talking about?"

"Sandellifer, of course. Has he not mentioned me? What a rude child he is!" Her low but clear laughter rang out over the garden. "I jest, young sir. Sandellifer is in all ways a most excellent wight, though I be his mother who says it."

I nodded, a little bewildered.

"But now we must become serious, for time passes even in this place. A storm gathers about you, young pooka. You have arrived like a cyclone in the 'midst of a delicately balanced dance of power, and like a cyclone, you are a wild and unknown element. None know where you shall strike, and uncertainty is despised among the older and greater powers. Many eyes are upon you."

"Me?" I choked out. "But why? I'm nothing, a nobody. Who would care what happens to me?"

"Do not deceive yourself, child. Few care about you – they concern themselves only with the change that you may beget. Precious few shall stand with you on the day of your proving, but those who do shall be dear friends indeed. Do not forget the risk they take in aiding your cause – it is no small thing they undertake."

I nodded, a little humbled. It crossed my mind for the first time that the three who had agreed to be my allies could just as easily have let me attack Braewynn alone, then challenged him when he was weakened from defeating me...if it weakened him at all.

"Meaning no disrespect, Lady Elenore, but why have you come here to tell me these things? What do you stand to gain from it?"

"Ah," she said, and smiled at me. "So the child is not entirely without reason and caution. Very good, young sir. The Sidhe give nothing without reason, and I have mine, which I believe I shall not share with you at this time. Suffice to say that you are allied with my son in this endeavor that you undertake; a mother's concern moves me to ascertain your nature, and I find it to my liking. Though you have lived a desolate life heretofore, it has taught you many things, and this pleases me. And so, I am minded to aid you in some small way, for both his sake and yours."

"Lady Elenore," I asked hesitantly, "Are you a queen? Why don't you stop Braewynn yourself, if he is a danger to your son?"

"You flatter me, young sir. Nay, not a queen, but the lady of an ancient and honorable house. I am Duchess of the realm of Agryvaine, and armsmistress to the Hame Dusksong. I am constrained, by great and binding oaths I undertook at the end of the great war, against moving directly against your foe, though I should be pleased to do so were I able. A debt exists between us, he and I."

I nodded, knowing that would be all I would get.

"Now our time in this place is ended. I ask that you grant me a boon, young sir. Should you do so, it shall not be forgotten by me and mine for a very long time. It is a simple request: I shall give you a thing that I wish you to carry with you at all times, never letting it leave your person, until this matter is resolved. On my honor, it will offer you no harm. Are we agreed on this?"

I knew, I knew, even as I knew that I was going to agree to her terms, that I was making a mistake. She'd said it herself – the sidhe give nothing without a reason. Still, I found myself agreeing, and even thanking her as she reached into one side of the cloak and drew out a small leather bag bound with a thong, and passed it to me.

"One last word may I give you, young Bryon, and it is this: Beware the seeming of those whom you have loved. Your foe is tricksome, and he will use the best of you to effect your defeat. Now go, and I will cover your retreat." With that, she stood suddenly and turned to look at the edge of the meadow behind me. Turning, I followed her gaze and spotted movement in the edge of the trees.

"Go now! Back through the door, and quickly!" She didn't wait to see if I was obeying, but turned and began to stride across the greensward, toward the dark shapes that were emerging from the trees.

I jumped to my feet and hurried to the door, which was still visible though seeming unconnected to anything at all...just a door in space. As I grasped the knob, I glanced back.

Lady Elenore had abandoned her concealing cloak, and strode across the lawn in full battle armor, it's crystalline surface acrawl with crackling blue light. In one hand she held up a shining globe, and in the other she grasped a long, slender, straight sword.

"Avaunt, unseelie scum! You trespass on Seelie land. Your purpose is discovered, and your foul intention foiled. Begone!" I heard Elenore's icy cold voice call out as I stepped through the door and closed it gently behind me.

I stood for a few minutes in the basement, leaning against the door and catching my breath. I couldn't seem to stop shaking, and I felt sick to my stomach. I realized that I still clutched the small leather pouch in my left hand. I was too dazed to even be curious about what it held, and I absently stuffed it in my pocket. Finally, I gathered myself enough to wander over to a sofa and sit down, before I fell down. So simple a thing, to walk through a door and nearly be caught. I knew that without Elenore's intervention, I'd probably be a guest in Braewynn's chamber of horrors tonight. Yet another debt owed…they seemed to be piling up.

After long minutes on the sofa, I finally pulled it together enough to stagger upstairs and wander back into the parlor where I'd met with my three hosts earlier this morning. Suddenly, a magazine about politics didn't seem like such a bad idea. I leafed through one of them again, and it wasn't much more interesting this time around than the last time. I sighed, lay down on the soft, overstuffed padding of the sofa and closed my eyes for a moment.

I awoke to the sound of someone singing in the kitchen. I was pretty bleary still, but when I heard the clock in the hall outside the parlor tolling the hours, I counted. 8pm? Damn, that was a power nap, for real.

The voice in the kitchen, which hadn't stopped when the clock started in chiming the hours, suddenly caught my attention again. It was a light and sweet tenor, singing Don McLean's old classic hit, American Pie. Not the soulless rendition that Madonna perpetrated, but the original version, with all the heart intact:

I met a girl that sang the blues,
and I asked her for some happy news,
but she just smiled and turned away.
So I went down to the sacred store
where I'd heard the music years before,
but the man there said the music wouldn't play…

Curious, I gathered myself and stood up, waited for the head rush to recede, and wandered out of the parlor in the general direction of the kitchen, following the voice.

"Hey, there you are, sleeping beauty. I thought I wouldn't be seeing you for a couple more hours. I considered waking you up when I got home, but you looked too cute sleeping, so I let it go." Sandy's voice was light and teasing.

"How could I sleep with all the racket you're making out here?" I said with a smile. "I bet Ralph is upstairs wondering what all the commotion is about."

Sandy just smiled back and said "Naw…he sleeps like the dead."

The counter top in front of the elf was covered with food… it looked like he'd bought the entire produce section at Safeway: carrots, plantain, starfruit, celery, fresh basil greens. On one side, the raw vegetables and fruit lay in colorful abandon, and on the other, bowls of carefully chopped, shredded and julienned produce rested where the chef had placed them, after they made their way across his cutting board. A huge stock pot sat on the stovetop behind the elf, already steaming gently and the source of the mouthwatering odor that had me sniffing appreciatively.

Sandy waved his knife at me carelessly. "Pull up a stool and have a seat, Bryon. We'll chat while I cook, and have a few slurps.

I just stood and stared for a moment. "Wow, this is amazing, Sandy. I don't think I've ever seen this much food in one place."

"Yes, well...have you ever tried cooking for just three? It's not worth the effort, really. If I'm going to cook, I like to get serious. Besides," he continued, his smile fading, "there's a lot of mouths to feed. In addition to dinner for us, I'm making a couple of pans of lasagna for a drop-in center for gay youth just down the street. Anything we don't eat will go to them as well, and there are a number of youngsters who come by here for a meal now and again. Nothing will be wasted, you can be sure.

"But enough seriousness...how was your day? Or did you sleep the whole day away?"

I felt a flush of guilt run through me – I knew I was going to have to tell him about going into the garden, but damn, that was one conversation I was not looking forward to. Still, if I'd learned anything in the last few years, it was that anything that looks hard just gets harder if it's put off. So, I sidled up to the counter across from him and leaned against it with one hip. He glanced up at me and flicked a smile at me before turning his attention back to his knife.

"Um...Sandy? Can I talk to you for a minute?"

"Sure. What's on your mind, Bryon?"

"Well, this is kind of serious. Could we sit down somewhere for a minute?"

He glanced at me, and without a word he set his knife down, wiped his hands on a dish towel, walked out of the kitchen and back down the hall to the parlor, and settled on a settee while I plopped down on the hassock. Now that I was actually doing it, I found it harder to start talking than I had thought it would be. For some reason, I felt like I'd betrayed his trust, and I wasn't liking that feeling at all – not even a little. He sat across from me and just watched me with curiosity, leaning forward a little so I'd know I had his full attention.

"Um…well, this morning…after you left to run your errands and all, I got kinda bored, so I thought I'd explore the house a little, you know? And…well, something kind of happened."

"Kind of happened?" he echoed. "What sort of 'kind of happened' are we talking about?"

"Uh, well…" I paused, and grimaced a moment. This wasn't going particularly well, and I knew it was about to get worse. "Not the good kind, I think."

"Mm. Why don't you tell me the details, and we'll figure it out after that, ok?"

I nodded, and wiped my suddenly sweating palms on my jeans. I glanced up at Sandy, but his face was neutral, waiting for me to continue. Did I say that things put off just get harder? Ignore me when I say things like that, ok?

"So I was kinda bored, and I decided to explore the house. I thought I'd start in the basement and work my way up, y'know? I figured it would be a good thing if I knew the layout of the house, cause ya never know what might happen, right?"

Sandy nodded, letting me know he was still with me, but his expression stayed carefully neutral.

"I wandered around down there for a little while, checking out the CDs, and then I went into the laundry room and checked out the machines and stuff…and I found this door. Which was kinda weird in itself, cause I hadn't noticed it from the other side of the wall, y'know? So I was kinda curious, and I opened it…and it led into this amazing garden place…"

To his credit, Sandy barely reacted to that – just arched an eyebrow at me and nodded for me to continue. So, I poured out the whole tale of my meeting with Lady Elenore, and all the events that followed, until I ended with waking up in this very same parlor and coming out to talk to him.

After I'd petered off into silence, he sat and stared at me for a moment, not saying a word. Somewhere in the telling, he'd shed his human seeming and now, as he got up to pace for a moment, his movements had taken on the inhuman grace of his true kind. He glided up and down the length of the room a couple times, then returned to the settee and settled down on it again. His green eyes were laser intent on my face when he spoke, but his voice was soft and didn't sound angry.

"So you found our back door, and had quite an adventure. Met my mother, eh? That's a meeting I would have paid money to see."

"I never felt like such a goof in my life," I admitted. "She's a little intimidating, isn't she?"

"She is that, and not one particle of it is put on. She's the real deal, boy-o. What you said about feeling like a goof? I still feel that way around her." He smiled a little at that, and I felt just a little bit better.

"But," he continued, "I think there's two more serious issues here. The first is this boon my mother asked of you, which in all fairness, you probably couldn't have turned down. May I see the pouch she gave you?"

I reached into my pocket and dragged it out. It was a small, black leather pouch with a leather drawstring, and a celtic triskeion painted on one side. I held it out for Sandy to take it, but he didn't. Instead he just stared at it for a moment, his eyes going sort of distant.

"Hmm...the bag itself is of human making – the sort of thing that any human with an interest in celtic culture might carry, and consequently won't draw attention from magic users like something made in Faerie might. Whatever is inside has a very passive, low level spell of concealment on it. If I didn't know it was something important, I'd never have noticed it at all. Very clever woman my mother is...unless someone was specifically looking for it, no one would ever know you carried it."

"But what is it?"

"I can't tell without opening the bag, and I'm not inclined to do that. All I can say is that if the Lady asked you to keep it close, I would. I trust her enough to be sure that she won't do anything that would harm us or our cause, and I know there is no love lost between she and Braewynn, so I think it's pretty safe for you to hold onto it."

"Then I will. Thanks for checking it out."

"Now, the last thing we need to talk about is the most serious. You said that she intercepted something or someone coming into the garden, and told you that they were Braewynn's minions, no?"

"Yeah... You should have seen her walking across the lawn, man. I was really glad I was not on the receiving end of that act."

"It wasn't an act, my friend. She's one of the Knight Commanders of Dusksong, and a powerful magic user as well. It would have taken a small army of bad guys to get past her. I know I'd never want to meet her in battle."

I just nodded. I still got the shivers when I thought about her striding across the lawn, sword in hand and challenging the baddies in her ringing voice.

"But the serious issue here is that this means your whereabouts is discovered. Braewynn knows you're here now, and who you're staying with. We'll have to have a conference with Ralph and Peter about this...they'll need to know what's going on."

It was going to be awhile until Ralph was awake, so I went back in the kitchen and helped with dinner. Well, 'helped' is probably the wrong word...I don't know a thing about cooking, and my experience of knives has been mostly as the subject, so I was relegated to washing and ripping salad and putting it in a big bowl. Even so, Sandy made sure to smile and compliment me on the work I was doing. Oddly, I didn't feel he was being condescending. He really thought I was doing good work.

After an hour or so, Peter wandered in and announced that Ralph was awake, and asked when dinner would be ready because he was hungry enough to start thinking about eating a Toyota. Sandy smiled and said it was ready except for a touch or two, and handed Peter a big platter with six roast chickens on it, asking him to carry it to the dining room. He handed me a bowl loaded with greens and asked me to follow Peter, and then come back for more.

By the time Ralph arrived, the table was loaded with bowls, platters and tureens, and the dining room smelled like heaven. There were four place settings at the table, each one with more spoons, forks, knives, glasses and extra plates than I had the slightest idea what to do with.

Before we started eating, Sandy poured some champagne in each of our glasses, and Ralph stood and raised his glass.

"First, to the cook. Second, to new friends..." and here he looked at me. "And finally, to the end of an evil that has needed it for a very long time."

"Hear, hear!" Sandy said, and sipped at his champagne. Peter took a big gulp of his and grinned widely. Ralph sipped his, and then switched to a goblet full of something very dark red and took a healthier swig of it.

I'd never tasted good champagne before, and it was quite a revelation. The flavors burst on my tongue and the bubbles tickled the back of my throat. I couldn't help smiling, and across the table Peter started to chuckle. I didn't feel too badly – he still had a big, goofy smile on his face too.

Dinner was…well, I don't really have the words for it. It was the best food I'd ever experienced. Ever. Nothing else even came in a close second. It took us three hours to eat, and the whole time, Sandy didn't say a word about the incident in the garden, or indicate in any way that he was worried.

Finally, when we'd finished eating, we each grabbed a last glass of wine and took them with us to the parlor. As we found seats and settled down, Sandy turned to Ralph.

"There's been a small change in our situation, and Bryon has another story to tell you. I think you'll enjoy this one as much as I did."

And so I found myself once more the center of attention as I retold the tale of my meeting with Lady Elenore, and watched Ralph's eyes go wide a little when I told the part about the boon. There was moment of silence when I finished, and I could see everyone else thinking about what it all meant.

"As to your meeting with the Lady, I don't know what to think," Ralph said slowly. "It's beyond my knowledge, but I don't think it is ill meant, or that whatever is in the pouch will hurt us or our cause. I think you should do as she asked, Bryon. Keep it close to you, and don't lose it."

I nodded agreement. His advice ran very closely to what I'd already decided.

"Now to the more serious business. Since we've been discovered, this means we need to move up our time line a bit. I'd hoped we'd have more time to discuss the ins and outs of the situation with Bryon so he'd really understand what is involved, but I'm afraid that luxury is gone. We're going to have to move ahead, and hope we don't misstep too badly."

"But that's a lot to expect, Ralph. He hardly knows us."

"I know, but we have to hope that he has seen enough of us to trust."

I sat on the overstuffed settee and felt like a spectator at a tennis match, with Ralph on one side of the net and Sandy on the other. I wasn't sure what they were talking about, but I knew that it somehow involved me, so I was kinda curious. Somehow I managed to keep my mouth shut until they'd come to an agreement that was clearly foregone. It seemed that whatever they were talking about was the only way to accomplish what they wanted to do. After a few more minutes, it boiled down to Ralph saying "So, do you want to ask him, or shall I?"

Sandy thought for a moment, and then said "I think I'd best do it. It might work to establish my right more deeply."

Ralph nodded, and waved a hand at Sandy, who turned to look at me. He gazed at me for a long moment, and then started.

"We have spent a great deal of time discussing this, Bryon, and it's the only way we can think of for this to work. The outcome we are looking for is that I will challenge Braewynn to a duel with a specific request that it be to death. In order for me to challenge Braewynn in such a serious way, he must have besmirched my honor as a knight of Seelie Court in some absolute manner. It is not enough that he has offered insult to you and that you asked me to act as your champion, because as a pooka you are officially nonaligned. The only way that this can become my fight is if the insult he offered you becomes as an insult offered to me. Do you follow me so far?"

I was pretty sure I could follow that. It meant that the only honor that counted in matters of dueling were those of members of either Seelie or Unseelie court and that seemed a little off base to me, but what did I know? I was just a renegade pooka, after all. So I nodded, and he went on.

"In addition to matters of court, there is an older system in place which is not practiced as much, but is still recognized by all the official powers: clans. Though much of the fey world has aligned themselves with either Seelie or Unseelie, there are a few instances of clan relations that cross the gap between the factions. You might not know it, but you're sitting in this room with one example: the three of us make up a clan all our own, duly recognized by the powers that be on both sides. Slider, as a redcap, is a member of a people who have declared for Unseelie. I, of course, am Seelie and Ralph is nonaligned. Normally this would be a problem, but since we have all claimed clan status, we've reached a solution. The commitment we made to the clan transcends our court allegiances, at least in day to day activities."

I had to think about that for a few minutes. It sounded like a pretty good deal, this clan thing...but if it was, why was it antiquated and why was nobody using it these days? There had to be more that he wasn't saying.

Sandy watched me and smiled. "I can see the doubt on your face, Bryon. If this whole thing is such a good deal, why has the Court system become the power that it is today? There has to be a catch, right?

"Well, there is. And it's a pretty big catch, I'd have to say. Clan is much more to the fey than it is to humans, Bryon. For us to declare clan kinship is to create a magical bond of great strength which can never be revoked once it is in place. It is permanent and inescapable. The only way to dissolve it is in death, and there are some who even question that statement, saying that clan kin are still bound after death. I don't know about that. But it is a very big step, and requires a deep knowledge of the ones you would bind yourself to. The ritual of binding itself involves opening oneself to the others who will share the bond: completely, inside and out. There are no secrets unrevealed, no thought that is not open for review by the others.

"Once the bond is complete, those who are part of the link will always know where one another are. They will feel the resonance of every pain and pleasure, every joy and sorrow that each member feels. They will know everything about one another, from the ground up."

"Jesus! That's what you guys have going on?" I blurted out. "No wonder no one wants to do it these days."

Sandy nodded. "Yes, it's what we, the three of us, share. And I have to tell you, sometimes it's like living without skin. But it works for us, and we're happy this way."

"To each their own, man. But why are you telling me this? What's it got to do with anything?"

Sandy paused, as if searching for the right words. "In order for you, a nonaligned entity, to challenge a member of Unseelie Court, you must have some connection to the Court system. At present, you don't. In a clan, dishonor and insult offered to one is dishonor and insult to all. Membership in a clan that included one who was of Seelie alignment would create that connection for you."

"At the cost of being tied to whoever else is in that clan for the rest of my life, right? And the man said 'no strings attached.' Huh, sounds like some pretty long strings to me."

"And yet," Ralph commented, "we offer it only as a proposition, and the binding works in the other direction equally as completely. Both parties are bound for life. This is the only way that we have been able to come up with for us to execute our intentions."

"During the ritual of binding, there is a period of three days of solitude and silence, in which each member must study what they have learned in the opening of their prospective clan kin," Sandy continued. "Agreement to the final binding cannot be coerced – it must be a free choice on the part of each. What I propose is that we perform the initial ritual of opening tonight, if all are agreeable, and then meditate upon what we all learn, and see if the final binding is what we want."

"Agreed," rumbled Peter.

Ralph tilted his head, looked at his feet and finally agreed as well.

Now they were all looking at me.

"Um…forever? No way to get rid of this thing?" I asked plaintively.

Sandy shook his head firmly. "Forever, Bryon. No going back, no second chances."

(5)

Well, shit. I knew going into this thing that I might owe them for the rest of my quite long life, but I hadn't even considered this kind of thing. Did I want to share everything about me with them? What if they were disgusted and horrified, and refused the binding after seeing what I was, what I had done? What if they didn't like me after seeing exactly who I was?

Then I had another thought: 'I'm not the only one involved here, am I? This involves the horse, too. Maybe I should be asking him what he wants.' And with that thought, a deep sense of approval welled up from somewhere within me.

"I'm going to need a moment, guys. I got somebody else I need to talk to about this. I won't be gone long."

Ralph looked a little startled by this announcement, but Sandy nodded approvingly and smiled a little, like I had passed a little test. I nodded back and then closed my eyes and leaned back in the chair. Relaxing my mind, I seemed to hover inside my skull for a moment and then dove deep down inside, to where the horse lived when we weren't living in his skin.

It's a dark place, full of pools of stagnant water and reeds, mist and fog blowing all over the place, and totally silent. I always arrive on a narrow, twisting little path right next to a big tree – a weeping willow that bends down over a wide pool, with the lowest boughs sweeping their tips in the water. I walked over to a big, gnarled root that stuck up above the muck and waited for him. I could feel him, a ways off but moving closer, coming fast. I'd be able to hear his hoofbeats any moment – there! Faintly, but getting stronger, I could hear the triple beat of his galloping hooves. He was almost close enough to feel his thoughts, not just his sense of presence…and now I could feel him completely. I felt my heart speed up with the sheer sense of power and freedom that he wore all the time, and just like I always did when I came down here, I wondered why I didn't just live in that unrestrained wonder all the time, why I kept trying to live as a two-legger in the the world of humans when I could be this, this unbound force of nature. It was an old line of thinking, and I had given up trying to make up a coherent answer.

I stood as he thundered up to me and reared high at the last moment, all flashing hooves and flying mane. He could have crushed me in that moment, but he never would and I knew it. We were brothers, and always would be.

As he returned to all fours and stood in front of me, I saw the wicked humor in his eyes just before he set his nose against my chest and pushed hard, sending me stumbling back to almost fall in the pond, but his head snapped forward at the last moment and his teeth latched onto my shirt, holding me from falling but not drawing me back to my balance, either. I laughed, grabbed his fetlock with both hands and held on as he hauled me back to my feet. I stepped up to his side as he waited patiently and vaulted up on his back, laying my head down on his neck and wrapping both arms around him, his mane rough against my cheek. He whickered at me, and then started off through the dark marsh, carrying me to the center of himself.

We were there almost before we started, it seemed. It wasn't a remarkable place, just a big, open spot beside a pool with a lot of lillies growing in it. I slid down off his back, and he turned his head to look at me with those glowing yellow eyes. He knew me, knew me in ways that no one else ever did, and still he loved me. I could feel it flowing off of him and into me: not just love, but honor at sharing a body with me, and pleasure in who I was becoming. It was an ineffable thing, his sense of love and approval. He knew me, he loved me, and woe to those who sought to harm me.

I thought to him all that Sandy had told me about clan bindings, and what it would mean to us, and found that he already knew of clan kin, and approved of such as a way to live. We were not meant to live alone, it seemed, and this was the way our kind should live. He knew that I would be the one to carry much of the burden of such a life, and he would leave the final decision to me, but he was not afraid of such a thing. From deep inside me, he had done his own checks on who these three were that proposed the idea, and it seemed to him they were three whom we could live with in harmony if we tried. But again, the final decision was mine, and he would live by it. I was humbled by his faith in me, even as I was proud that he believed in me to such a degree. He did, however, want to talk to the three for a moment, using my voice. We had done this before on occasion; I was not included in the conversation except as a bystander, so it always made me a little nervous, but I agreed.

At the next moment, I was gently moved to one side in my own head, and I watched as my body suddenly straightened and then rose to its feet, facing the three of them. My eyes had gone from their usual hazel green to shining pure yellow and pupil-less. When he spoke, the horse's voice was deep and gravelly – nothing like my own tenor.

"I am Dubhain," I/he said. "I am he who shares a body with Bryon, and I know you. I have watched and heard all that has happened. You seem honorable and fair, yet such seeming may hide great wickedness."

Sandy rose to his feet a moment later, and bowed deeply to me/him. "Hail, Dubhain. It is an honor to meet you, at last. There is no seeming here – we are what we are. I would extend the offer of clan kin to you as well as Bryon, and I hope that you will be a part of the opening that I propose we perform. I would have you know me, and all of us, that you may decide on a course of action that will support your honor."

I/he stared at Sandy for a moment, and then replied "Honor is for the Lios Alfar, knight of Seelie. I know no such thing. I know love, and I hold it for one only, for Bryon. He knows my thoughts on what you propose, and shall reveal them in time. Know this, all of you: the bonds of clan kin will not save you, should you betray Bryon. If you prove untrue, you will face me."

The next moment, I was back in control and sinking onto the hassock. I was weary to the bone, as I always was after letting Dubhain (now why hadn't he told me his name was Dubhain before? From deep down I could hear some definitely equine snickering, and then silence) speak in my place.

"Welcome back, Bryon. I was wondering when we would meet your partner. I must say, he's a horse of few words, but those he speaks are potent." Sandy was looking very serious, but suddenly smiled a little. "I think he's struck both Peter and Ralph dumb, something I didn't think anything could accomplish."

"He's impressive, isn't he?" I said proudly. 'And he's my brother, and he loves me!' I wanted to add, but I held that thought in, and felt the warmth of affirmation from within me.

93

"Well, that was interesting," Ralph remarked, shaking his head a bit. "I don't believe I've ever encountered anything quite like that before. So, Dubhain said that you know his thoughts concerning our proposal – might we know what he thinks, as he will obviously be party to any agreements we make?"

"He thinks it's not a bad idea, and that this kind of bonding is how we're supposed to live, if it can be made with the right people. He's kind of old school that way. He never liked the whole Court system, it seems. He says it leaves too much room for shenanigans."

"Which the clan system does not," Ralph replied, nodding his head. "Well then, I think it is time to call the question. Shall we do the opening ceremony, and if we do it, shall we do it now – tonight? I say aye. What say the rest of you?"

"Aye." Peter's deep voice held confidence in the choices his brothers would make.

"Aye," said Sandy. "I think we have taken stock of our proposed kinsman, and seen that he is good. I am ready to see if we are right."

Staring around at them, I knew it was something I would have to do. There was no other hope for me – for us, Dubhain and I – so we would have to risk all on a single gambit. I nodded, and tried to make my voice as firm as possible. "Aye. We do it."

"Then we are in agreement, and the ceremony shall go forward," Ralph said quietly. "Wisdom and good fortune to all of us in the coming hours."

It didn't feel like wisdom or good fortune over the next few hours. Suddenly I felt sort of irrelevant, as Sandy sprang into action and recruited the other two to help. I was told to get some rest, as it would take at least two hours for the preparations for the ceremony to be complete, and further told to hold all my questions until the actual event, because they would all be answered then; besides, couldn't I see that they were busy? This last was said by Ralph with a little grin on his face, so I sighed and took myself off to bed for a couple hours rest until they came to get me. As I slept, my head was full of the sound of galloping hoofbeats.

(6)

I awoke suddenly, to the feel of Peter's hand on my shoulder. "Come on," he rumbled. "Sandy says it's time."

I nodded, and followed him out of the room, down the stairs and into the parlor, where all the furniture had been removed and the rug rolled back to expose the hardwood floor. What the rug had hidden was a large circle of dark red wood inlaid into the blond hardwood of the floor, and inside this dark red circle, another circle of shining golden runes seemed to float slightly above the floor. Sandy, still in human seeming, stood on the other side of the circle from me, and Peter stepped away from me to the left side of the circle, opposite where Ralph stood at my right.

"Brothers, we seek to know another who would join us in clan kinship, and to be known by him. Do we all seek this of our own will, freely and without coercion?"

"Aye," Peter and Ralph said together, in almost one voice. As I watched, a slight brightening of the runes ran all the way around the circle, the whole circle flared slightly as the brightness finished its round, and then the whole thing settled to its previous muted glow.

"Bryon, what you see before you is a Circle of Truth. If you agree to be bound by it as we have, you will be unable to speak falsehood or to prevaricate on any question placed before you, even as we cannot. Nothing less than absolute truth will pass your lips while bound to this circle, nor will dishonest thought be allowed. Will you be so bound?"

"I will," I said steadily. Now that I had made the decision, it was time to get on with this. The moment I said it, a deep chime rang in my mind, and I knew that my answer had been noted by the spell, and I was now bound to its power.

"Very well, then.The time for acceptable seemings is past, brothers. In this place of truth, we should be what we are and no less." With that, Sandy shed his human mask and stood proudly in his elven self…and naked. I don't know why that was such a surprise to me – wouldn't we all be naked to each other in just a moment, in far more important ways than just our bodies? Still, I was a little taken aback. I suppose it had to do with exposing my body to so many over time, and wanting to preserve something of myself from that. But this was not the time for holding back. I kicked off my shoes and stripped out of my clothes, to stand naked in front of them.

Strider had removed his amulet and the rest of his clothes, and stood in the all together to my left. His hugely muscled frame was covered with hair, almost fur, and his wide mouth hung slightly open, revealing row upon row of razor teeth. He smiled a little at me, but I knew his intent and didn't shudder.

Ralph, meanwhile, had also removed his clothing and his human guise. He was taller and more slender, and his skin shone white and faintly luminescent. His hair was even more wild than usual, and grew part way down his spine in a sort of mane. His pupils glowed crimson and feral, and I could see the hunger that he always fought in that burning redness.

It was at that moment that I realized there was a presence at my back. I glanced back and saw a huge, black, four-legged shadow looming over me – Dubhain, come to stand at the circle. I wouldn't stand alone in this trial, it seemed, and that was a comfort.

"In a moment," Sandy said, drawing my attention back to the business at hand, "I will start the incantation of opening that is also the initial sequence of the Clan binding. When the incantation is complete, each of us will experience the lives of all the others in the circle. It will not play out before us as if it were a movie: we will experience it first hand, and know all the pain and disappointment, the joy and triumphs that have made each of us what we are. Are there any questions?"

There was a moment of silence. Each of us knew that we had come too far for questions, at this point.

"Very well, then. Let us begin."

I'd never heard an elf sing before, let alone one who was reckoned to be among the best of his kind. It made my heart pound in my ears, and I could feel his voice resonating in my bones. There were times when I could swear I wasn't hearing his voice with my ears at all, but that my soul was receiving the sound directly. As he sang the opening phrases, Sandy began to glow a pale golden color. As his voice soared through the ensuing sections, the color grew deeper and stronger, till it shone out of his whole body and it seemed that his flesh became translucent with the building power. At the same time, it seemed that he was standing in a whirlwind that effected only him, as his hair rose and swirled about his head and his lifted arms.

I was transfixed, fascinated by the purity and beauty of his voice, unrestrained as it was by the removal of his human seeming. I don't know how long it took him to sing all the parts of the spell, but it seemed to go on and on, with definite sections and parts all interweaving, with themes disappearing and reappearing seemingly at random, but always blending into a complete wholeness. Finally, after a long, crescendo-ing series of phrases, he finished. There was one moment of perfect, crystalline silence, and then it happened.

The year was 978 a.d. Hakam the Second ruled in Cordoba, and the land was at peace, save in the north where the remnants of the christian kingdoms battled on. Abduraman was young, handsome and in love with his beautiful wife, Relillia. They had been married only 2 months before, in their native city of Toledo. Both of their fathers were craftsmen in the guild of arms makers, and their future looked bright.

In the fall of that year, a man came to the father of Abduraman to commission a blade. He was willing to pay a handsome price, and so the blade was crafted, and Abduraman given the task of delivering it. The terms of the sale specifically stated that the delivery must happen after nightfall, and so it was that the young man walked through the streets of the city in the darkness, finally reaching the home of the patron in a wealthy section of the city.

Tapping at the gate of the compound, Abduraman was admitted to the courtyard and ushered into the house. It was there that he met the man who had commissioned the blade: Ibn Al-hamid, a notoriously reclusive scholar and merchant prince of the city.

In a beautifully appointed sitting room, Ibn asked to see the blade he had purchased. Abduraman carefully unwrapped the swaddling cloths around it, and then displayed it to the man, offering him the hilt that he might try its balance. The man commented favorably on its exquisite workmanship, and the delicate balance it possessed. Then, stepping closer to Abduraman, he suddenly stiff-armed the young man back against the wall and then drove the sword through his shoulder, pinning him to the wall. As the young man screamed in agony, Ibn stepped closer yet, gripped Abduraman's hair in one hand and yanked his head back. Without a word, he bent his mouth to the young man's exposed neck and suddenly elongated teeth sheared through Abduraman's skin and into the large arteries and veins of his throat; blood fountained out of the severed vessels, gushing into the open mouth of Ibn, who drank deeply and ruthlessly of the young man's vitality.

When Abduraman's blood was nearly drained, and his heart fluttered at the ragged edge of failure, Ibn carefully opened a vein in his own wrist and set the young man's mouth to it, instructing him to drink. He did, and so set out on a journey that would be both long and unexpected. It began the next night when he woke in Ibn Al-Hamid's bedchamber, and learned the way of a master vampyre with his subordinates. It was both horrifying and fascinating to the young muslim, who had heard of such things but never imagined he would be involved in them. Strangely, he learned something of himself in that time.

On a certain night two months later, having been deliberately starved by his master and gripped by an extremity of hunger, Abduraman returned to his home and slaughtered his wife Relillia, her father and mother, and his own father who happened to be there when he arrived. Sated on their blood, he slept. Awakening, he realized what his blood madness had brought him to and fled the city, wandering for many years through medieval europe. He never escaped the guilt and pain of his first kills, and lived a life overshadowed by this pain, a life apart from his people.

Even as I lived the incident in moorish Iberia, my consciousness split and I became another, this one a young elf.

"Mother, I must leave. I have brought dishonor to our House, and though I count it no dishonor to love, those who have power over us do not agree. I would not see my own dishonor stain you."

"Sandellifer, you are the child of my body, my only son. What do I care for the rantings of witless old men when they would separate us? You will never be a source of dishonor to me – you know this to be true. Love whom you will, but stay and be a knight of Agryvaine."

"You know that I cannot. Already the challenges have begun, as word of my liaison with Alreid spreads. I can defeat these challengers, but how many must I fight? Will I fight duels every day for the rest of my life?"

"In time, the furor will pass. What of Alreid? Why does he not stand at your side?"

"Ah, well…Alreid…has decided that his path lies elsewhere and declares that he was the victim of coercion. I will not honor the lie with a defense. If one of us must be dishonored in the eyes of the Court, let it be me. He is not strong, Mother. He could not bear it."

"So be it, though saying it rends my heart. What will you do?"

"I will seek other lands, and other peoples. Perhaps somewhere I will find tolerance and peace, a place where the dominion of the Lios Alfar holds no sway."

"I would gainsay you if I could, my son, but you are a man grown. I have taught you all the skills of sword and magic that I posses – they must suffice to keep you alive in whatever strange places you find yourself. Though we speak of it not often, know that you have your mother's love, respect and care, and do not hesitate to call on me should you find yourself in need. I will not fail to answer, you may be sure. Know also that the hearth and threshold of Agryvaine are always open to you, should you decide to return."

To his mother's shock and bemusement, the young elf stepped forward and clasped her close in his arms, embracing her long and tightly. When he loosened his grip, he moved back a little and placed a single kiss on each of her cheeks.

"Good bye, Mother." Without a look back, the disgraced young knight walked out into the courtyard, mounted the charger his mother had given him all those years ago, and rode out of the fortress. At the border of Faerie, he turned his mount loose, knowing it would return to his mother's castle, and set out on foot. He would arrive in human lands some time later, and begin a life apart from his people.

And even as I lived out the disgrace and self-exile of the young elf, my mind was split a third way, and...

He howled in pain, but submitted to the beating laid upon him by the ruler of his motley. He had failed to bring home food yet again, and he deserved to be beaten for his failing. But even as the chief of his motley beat him with a cudgel and kicked his body when he fell down, the pain in his heart nearly eclipsed the agony of broken ribs and fractured limbs. He knew that no matter how he was beaten, or how much food he brought to the motley, he was changed, and no longer belonged. An irrevocable change had happened to him, though he'd hardly noticed it at the time. He knew that he could not accept the offer of the older female of the other motley to take him as mate, not though his chief commanded it. He had another, a human male – the shame of it tore at him even as he was beaten viciously – and there could be no one else, though it cost him everything.

When at last the beating ended, and his chief asked him in a quiet voice if he planned to bring honor to his motley by accepting the older female's suit, he stared at his chief, the father of the motley, the one who held the power of life and death over him, and denied him.

"Then you are no longer of us. I name you stranger, and I cast you from among us. Go, and do not return lest you nourish the tribe with your body," the chieftain growled. One by one, all who had gathered to witness turned their backs on him, and he was alone – bereft of comfort, and already dead in his own mind. Undone. He left, slinking away to what he expected to be his death, but instead became the beginning of a life apart from his people.

All these events and a great multitude more I lived through, experiencing the lives of the other three. Dimly, somewhere far away, I was aware of tears leaking from my eyes and dripping from my chin to the floor.

Finally, having seen all there was of each one, I surfaced back into my own mind. Overwhelmed by the pain I had experienced in Sandellifer's shame, Slider's despair, and Ralph's guilt, I fell to the floor, sobbing in misery. How could they stand it?

As I lay there, lost in misery and pain, I almost missed the gentle, supporting strength that rose from within me. The voice in my mind was unmistakable, though – the deep, rough voice of Dubhain.

"Come brother, they have shown us all. Now you must be strong and show them your face, standing on your own legs. Come, stand up."

From somewhere, I found the strength to stand and turn to the three of them – still naked, still in their fey, true selves. I didn't see them as I had before, though. They were no longer a strange grouping, an oddity that might be able to offer me help. I saw them as a unity, three who had suffered terribly and taken the strength from it to forge the bonds that I saw between them now: a golden light arcing from one to the other, weaving in and about them till they were surrounded by bands of light.

As I stood and stared at them, the light surrounding them began to fade, and soon I was looking at three men, naked and unembarassed, and all looking at me sadly. There was something else on each of their faces, but I didn't recognize it. I hadn't seen much compassion in my life.

Finally, Sandy broke the silence. "I imagine you're a bit tired, Bryon. You should go and get some sleep. You'll have the next three days to contemplate what you learned, and then we shall need your answer and inform you of our decision as well. But, that's for another day. For now, a few hour's sleep, I think."

I nodded and started out of the room towards the stairs and up to my little bedchamber on the third floor. As I gripped the doorknob, I paused and looked back. I felt my heart lurch with longing at what I saw.

The three of them – elf, vampyre and redcap – stood in a tight group in the middle of the room. All of them had their arms about each other, sharing warmth and strength. I heard deep, hiccuping sobs from Slider, as the other two stroked his hair and kissed him, sharing the comfort of their presence.

'I could have that,' I thought briefly. 'All I have to do is reach out for it, and it's mine.' With that, I left them there and went to bed.

(7)

When I woke up the next morning, it seemed like any other morning for a minute, and then suddenly the events of yesterday crashed into my mind. Instead of getting up to put on my sweats and wander downstairs like I had been going to do, I lay back into the warmth of the down comforter and thought about all of it for a time, not really trying to make sense of it, just wandering among the memories that I had lived through.

The common experience that bound them all was pretty obvious. They all loved other men, and found that it was unacceptable to the societies they lived in. I had lived the memories of Ibn bringing Abduraman – who would later change his name to Ralph after the reconquest of the Iberian peninsula by the christians – to knowledge of his inner self. Brutal lessons, but Ralph had long ago let the shame he'd felt over the rape of his mind and body go, knowing that harboring such would only poison him further.

And poor Slider! Jesus, to be cast out like that, and he hadn't even done anything with this guy he fell in love with. I realized, as I lay there, that it had been Slider's crisis that was the catalyst for creating their relationship, but that it was not his need that kept them together. With support and caring from the other two, Slider had recovered and become the third, balancing leg of the group. How would the family balance when Dubhain and I were added in?

And suddenly, I stopped. I needed to take another look at that thought. *When*, not *if*. It came to me, in that moment, that I had already decided. I didn't need three days to think about it. These guys, as Dubhain had said, were guys that I could live with. I had never really wanted anyone else around for more than a night in the last many years, since that day I stood on the dock in Leschi, staring out over the gray-green water of the lake, and taking my clothes off so they wouldn't get wet. And now, I wanted it. I wanted to be family, like they were.

What the hell was I thinking? I didn't even know if they wanted me, or not. Maybe they were disgusted by me...but as I looked back over the memories I had lived, I was pretty sure they weren't disgusted. I remembered the odd look on each of their faces, and though I didn't know what it was, it didn't look like a bad thing. Dubhain wasn't saying anything either way, just lending me the quiet support I always felt from him when we weren't talking. How would they accommodate the two of us, with our odd habits and unexpected conversations? I smiled, imagining Ralph's face when I told him that we would need a pool in the backyard.

I lay my head back on the pillows and closed my eyes. Thinking is harder work than it should be, you know. Just as I was slipping away, I heard the rumble of Dubhain's voice for the first time that day. I was so close to sleep that I wasn't sure what he said, but it sounded like "Not two. One." It didn't make any sense, and I fell off the edge into sleep right at that moment.

I woke up again in the mid-afternoon. I lay there in bed and listened to the silence of the house. Ralph would be upstairs sleeping, and Sandy could be out in the yard, gardening. He seemed to like grubbing about with plants and dirt, for some reason. My stomach was grumbling about how many hours it had been since I filled it, so I got up, pulled on a pair of sweats from the little chest of drawers that Sandy had filled with clothes for me, and wandered out of my room and down the stairs to the main floor. I figured with all the food we'd had last night, there must be some left overs I could scrounge.

As I walked into the kitchen, I glanced out the window to see what kind of day it was. The window overlooked the front garden, and then out over Aloha street at the front of the house. I was so busy taking a look at the weather that I didn't notice at first that there were two people standing just outside the front gate, looking up at the house like tourists on their first day in the city. When it finally registered that they were there, I felt a shock of recognition go right through my whole body. I stared, unable to believe my eyes. It was my foster parents, from all those years ago! What the hell were they doing here, right outside the house? I wanted to hide and ignore them, but I also wanted to go out and explain, let them know that I wasn't dead, as they must have thought. With hardly a thought, I darted to the front door and peered out through the little glass portal in the solid oak. Yes, it was them! They'd hardly changed at all. I knew I had to go out and talk to them. Maybe they wouldn't recognize me, and I could just chat with them for a bit. Or something.

Hardly stopping to think, I grabbed Sandy's leather coat that hung on a peg by the door, and hurried out to see the two of them. They seemed to be admiring the house, pointing out the details to each other and talking quietly. As I came out the door, I saw them both look at me, and they started to move away. I walked briskly up the walk to the gate and looked both ways along the street, pretending I was looking for someone. The two of them had paused, and looked like they were about to speak to me, so I looked up and down the street for another second. Sure enough, the woman who had been my foster-mom smiled at me.

"Excuse me, do you live in this house? We were just commenting on how much we admired it."

I smiled back at her warmly. She had always been so sweet to me when I was in her care, and the memory of her had always been something I clung to in the darker periods of my life. I tried to keep my voice casual and light. I didn't want to give myself away.

"Well, my friends own the place. I'm a house guest at the moment. Would you like to step inside the gate for a tour of the garden?"

Smiling, my former foster dad demurred. "Oh no, we couldn't. I'm sure you've got things to do, and we don't want to take up your time like that."

"It's no bother for me. I'm sort of at loose ends today, so..."

Still smiling at the man, I heard the woman say "Oh, my dear god. Is it possible?" Both the man and I turned to her, he out of curiosity and I with a sinking feeling. So much for going unrecognized.

"What is it, Jane? What's the matter?" the man asked, looking a little concerned at her blanched face and the tears starting out of her eyes.

"Erik, don't you recognize him? Don't you see who he is?"

"Who...who is, Jane? What are you talking about?"

"Him, Erik. It's Bryon, little Bryon from all those years ago. It is you, isn't it, Bryon? Oh, how is this possible? We thought you were dead!"

"Oh my god, Jane – you're right. Look, we have to calm down. We don't want to scare him. He probably doesn't even know who we are."

Well, now I was torn. I didn't know whether to play dumb and just act like I didn't know what they hell they were talking about, or own up and maybe come away with some friends, if they wanted that. They were two of the few people who had ever treated me like they cared in my whole life, and deep down I wanted to know them. After a moment, I decided 'what the hell' and just said, "Yeah, I'm Bryon. I'm sorry for the way I just left you guys back then."

"I can't believe this. Where have you been all this time? We found your note, and then we found your clothes on the dock, and…" Jane was looking at me like she'd just found the holy grail. It made me a little uncomfortable, but I figured there would be a little awkwardness to start with, so I tried to ignore the discomfort and answer the question.

"Well, I've been living here and there, doing a few odd jobs to get by, you know. It's been ok."

"Thank god! It was so hard back then, thinking that we'd failed you somehow, and then Dan cut us off and moved out right after that. It was hard to lose both of you so close together." I could see Erik trying to keep it together, trying to stay calm, but he was losing it too. It was pretty clear, as much as I had learned to read people. He turned away a little, not wanting me to see him cry. I felt so bad, knowing that I was the reason he was crying.

"I'm sorry I didn't come back and tell you I was ok. It just felt better to make a clean break, somehow…"

"Well, never mind that. I'm just so glad we found you again. You've become such a handsome young man, hasn't he, Erik?"

My foster dad's eyes were rimmed with red, but he was looking at me and nodding his head. "You've grown into a fine young man, Bryon. I'm glad to see you looking so well."

"Bryon, we were just on our way to get a little lunch. Perhaps you'd like to join us, so we can sit down and talk? I don't want to pressure you, but this has been so overwhelming, I really need to process this."

I smiled a little at that. I still remembered her saying things like that about 'processing' things from when I was a little. I'd never known what she meant back then, but I understood now. It sounded like a good idea…we surely had a lot to process.

"Um, ok. I'll need to run in and put on some real clothes, but if you'd like to wait on the porch for a minute, I can run in and change and be right back."

"We'll just wait for you here, Bryon. Hurry though – I can't wait to talk to you."

I nodded and walked swiftly back up the walk to the house, ran up to my little room and threw on a pair of clean jeans, a polo and a pair of sneaks, and was heading back out when I ran into Peter at the bottom of the stairs.

"Where ya going, Bryon? You're not supposed to leave the house, y'know. It's not really safe."

"I know, Peter, but I met up with these friends that I haven't seen in years, and they invited me out to lunch. I really need to talk to 'em, so I'll be back in a little while. It's ok – they're safe."

"I don't think this is a very good idea, Bryon – " But before he could finish the thought, I was out the door and hurrying down the walk toward Jane and Erik. I'll admit I was a little excited – I'd dreamed more than once about this happening, and now here it was.

"Ah, here you are!" Erik exclaimed when I hopped over the gate and onto the sidewalk beside them. "We planned on going to the Canterbury, but I think this calls for something a little more elegant, don't you Jane? How about Bistro Parisienne? It's a little pretentious, but the the food is pretty good." With a broad smile and a quirked eyebrow, he looked at Jane and I, and we were both nodding. "Well, that's that then. To the Bistro!"

With one of them on each side of me, we started off down the street. We'd gone about fifty feet when I turned to talk to Jane and suddenly it felt like the world had collided with the back of my head. I went out with a flash of stars in front of my eyes, and everything got black.

I wasn't out long. That's one thing about being a pooka – there's always one of you that doesn't get knocked out and can wake up the one that does. So when I came to about 5 seconds later, I was justifiably a little confused. I looked up at a grinning Erik, who was busily applying a plastic binder to my wrists like the police use instead of cuffs sometimes, and I felt someone – it had to be Jane – grabbing my ankles and pulling them together to tie them up too. Suddenly my attention was drawn away when something bellowed from just down the street. It sounded really big, and really angry. I hoped it wasn't after me, 'cause I was in deep enough doo without adding whatever was coming.

Jane and Erik both stopped what they were doing and looked up just in time to see Peter come hurtling over the gate and start down the sidewalk toward us at full speed. And man, could that guy move. I'd always thought he was kinda big and ponderous, but when he needed to get somewhere, he could flat out move.

The second they saw him, the two – who I had figured out by now were not my real foster parents – cut loose with a pair of levin bolts that sizzled as they left their hands and arced out towards Peter like lightning. One he dodged, but the other one winged him on the shoulder, and it broke his stride. He paused and glared at the two of them, reached into his shirt and fished out the pendant, lifted it over his head and suddenly he was not a big, burly guy, but a full on redcap, with a look on his face that would have curdled fresh milk.

The two who had captured me dropped their glamours as well, and suddenly I was laying on the ground at the feet of two goblins, not the foster parents I thought I had found. I closed my eyes in shame – dear gods, I was a sap. All they had to do was play to my little orphan andy fantasies, and they took me like a sleeping pigeon.

Goblins are tough and mean, sort of the thugs of the elder kin. They can use enough magic to make them pretty deadly, in addition to having pretty good hand to hand skills. These two were middling tall, with leathery grey skin and black hair pulled back into topknots at the back of their heads. Their mouths were wide and filled with needle-like teeth. The way they moved it was pretty obvious they had fought together a lot – they were smooth and coordinated, and they took the fight right to Slider. They each pulled a dagger on their way to him, and it was starting to look pretty bad. I wanted to get up and help, but my hands were tied; I didn't have any castable magic, so I'd have to fight hand to hand, and I wasn't much good at it as a guy. Still, I was working my hands in the plastic restraint, trying to get free when the three of them met.

They reached him, and suddenly one of the goblins shrieked horribly. It stopped and stared down at its arm that had been holding the dagger, but which now ended about midway up its forearm. The other piece of it was in Slider's mouth, having been bitten cleanly off. He chewed twice and swallowed, and then spat the dagger out on the ground. The wounded goblin bent forward over his maimed arm, and I could see Slider's mouth opening again with the aim of taking the goblin's head off at the shoulders, when he suddenly grunted in pain and froze, then turned to stare down at his side. The other goblin's dagger was buried to the hilt in the redcap's side, just below his ribs.

"Slider!" I yelled. I'd scrambled to my feet by now and was running to throw myself on the goblin to prevent him from pulling the dagger out and finishing it, but someone else beat me to the punch. A dark aura abruptly sprang into being around the goblin's upper body, it shrieked in agony, and then the lower half of its body fell sideways and landed on the sidewalk. The upper half was completely gone as the dark aura faded and Sandy stepped forward. With a gesture, he froze the remaining, wounded goblin and hurried forward to Slider, who was still crouched and staring at the dagger stuck in his side.

Sandy turned and looked over at me. "Help me get him in the house."

"What about those two?" I gestured at the goblins. He stared at them coldly, then muttered a word and waved at them, and they disappeared.

"Hurry, we've got to get him inside. He needs healing, and quickly. That dagger was spelled." With another quick gesture he freed my hands from the plastic binder, and I jumped forward to help him lift Slider to his feet.

Slider groaned deep in his throat as we moved him, and he'd broken out in a sweat. His face was twisted in a rictus of deepest pain. What the hell was the spell on that dagger?

As if reading my mind, Sandy said "It's an agony spell. It causes massive pain. I'm damping it as best I can, but it's an Unseelie spell and doesn't respond very well to what I can do."

I nodded like I understood, but I didn't have a clue what was going on.

Sandy ignored me after that, talking quietly to Slider and assuring him that all would be well. We dragged him up the sidewalk and into the house, and laid him out on the floor in the entryway.

"What did you do with the goblins?" I asked.

"Sent them back to their master," he replied with some satisfaction in his voice. "It'll give him something to think about before he tries this sort of thing again."

I didn't ask any more questions. Instead, as he worked over Slider and tried to stop the bleeding and hold the spell in check, Sandy asked me one. "Why didn't you change out there? You'd have been able to get out of the binder, and been a lot more help."

Stung a little by this, I answered back a little more hotly than I meant to. "How could I? There was no water."

He looked up at me, clearly surprised. "Water? I hadn't heard that water had anything to do with it."

"I can only change in water. I don't know why...Isn't that just part of being a pooka?"

"Huh," he grunted, and then turned back to what he was doing. It took a while, but finally he was able to unwind the pain spell. The look of relief on Slider's face was very, very good to see, though he hadn't said anything the whole time Sandy was working on it. Once he had that part worked out, the rest was easy. Sandy placed his hand on Slider's side, his fingers spread out all around the entry wound, gripped the dagger with the other hand, and healed the wound as he slipped the knife out. He glanced at me and we both helped the redcap to his feet, and suddenly he hugged Slider tightly.

"Damn you, brother, how many times have I told you not to bite off more than you can chew? When are you going to learn to wait a second until I can get there? I can't have your back if you won't wait."

"I was just softening 'em up for ya a little."

"A piece of advice: next time, don't. We take them together, or not at all. Got it?"

Slider looked at his brother and smiled. "Got it. And thanks for helping with the spell — it was kinda sore."

Sandy turned and looked at me then. I was expecting anger, but his eyes were mild. "I'd like your word that you won't leave the house without at least taking one of us with you, Bryon. We are bound by our honor to protect you, and you put us in a very difficult position if you leave by yourself."

I nodded fervently. "For sure, Sandy. With one of you, or not at all. You got it."

"Good. Now, who's hungry? Anybody worked up an appetite from that little exercise?"

Slider looked interested, but I just shook my head. I needed some time alone to process what had just happened.

Nothing more was said about the incident after that. I walked around with my tail between my legs for a day or so, until

I figured out that the three of them really didn't blame me for what had happened. I worried constantly, wondering what Braewynn's next move against me would be, but the next two days passed uneventfully.

Exactly seventy two hours after the opening ceremony of the clan binding ritual had happened, we were once again gathered in the parlor around the red circle, this time to confirm our decisions on whether to proceed or not. I was filled with hope and dread, both in anticipation of an affirmative answer. If they chose against me I would be lost, so I wasn't even thinking about that possibility.

The singing in this ritual was four part, because all of us would be involved. I'm not much of a singer, but Sandy had coached me on what I would need to do, so I croaked through my part. Ralph sang his part in a surprisingly strong baritone, and Slider had – as I had expected – a deep basso profundo voice that seemed to extend down right to the bottom of my hearing threshold. Well, ok…not really, but if giant boulders had voices, they might have sounded like he did. I had no idea what the words I sang in the ancient language of the incantation meant exactly, but they seemed to satisfy the requirements.

The circle of runes inside the dark red circle was blue this time, shining deep and pure in the half-light of the parlor. I could see the other three, standing naked and proud at the other quarters of the circle, and I felt like I might faint as I waited for their decision.

"Brothers, we have looked upon this man and seen what he is, and what he has been. Likewise, he has seen us through and through. We have pondered long and hard on what we have seen. Bryon and Dubhain, have you reached a decision? What say you?"

I paused for a moment. My answer here would shape the rest of my life, and there would be no backing away from this, ever. I swallowed hard, forced my anxiety back and made the only answer I could.

"Yes. Dubhain and I would join you in clan binding. We want to be your brothers, to support and defend the clan with all that we are even to our death, if you want us." I felt the depth of affirmation in Dubhain's presence at my back, and knew that he believed I had made the right decision. Again, I heard the chime in my mind as my decision was noted by the spell.

Sandy's voice went on. "And Slider, what is your decision?"

"He's a good boy, Sandy. I like 'im, and I think he could be good for us. I say we take him." Whew, one down and only two more to go. I could feel the sweat beading on my forehead, and my eyes were stinging with it.

"Ralph, have you reached a decision?"

"I have, Sandy. Like Slider, I believe that Bryon is a good man at heart. Even with all that has happened to him, he has never committed an evil act against others, though his care for himself has been less than exemplary. I think he will become a formidable man in time, and I would be there to see it happen. So yes, I agree to his joining the clan."

"I, as well, have come to a decision on this matter. His way has been long and painful to this point, but it has forged in him a strength and will that will bolster our own. I say, be welcome Bryon and Dubhain. You are kin of the Clan of the Red Circle, by word of all its members and by your own decision."

At those words, the blue glyphs on the floor blazed up high and filled the room with light. I closed my eyes, but it was shining inside my head, permeating every particle of my being. A part of me that I had never even known was empty suddenly filled till I felt like I might split open all over the room, and there was such painful pleasure in the feeling that I longed for it to happen. Like a physical touch on my skin, I could feel the others in this new bonding. It was overload, and I felt tears running down my cheeks again. As I stood there and tried to deal with the feeling, I didn't even know that the others had stepped forward until I felt their hands and arms around me, holding me close in that way that I had longed for that night – gods, was it only three days ago? It seemed like a lifetime.

I heard Sandy murmuring somewhere above my head, his voice full of laughter. "Freaks and Fags Forever, brothers. And now we are four…no wait, is it five? I don't know. Any road, haven and hospitality no longer, Bryon – you're one of us."

Dimly I heard Dubhain's voice rumble "Four. We are one, though he knows it not." I was a little puzzled, but I let it go. I'd need to ask about that later, I thought, and then promptly forgot all about it.

(8)

We spent the next couple of hours talking and drinking coffee, and everyone seemed to be ignoring that it was the wee hours of the morning. Ralph had put some light jazz on the CD player and it played quietly away in the background as we talked and laughed and teased each other. After the solemnity of earlier, it was a relief to simply sit and chat, and I felt a strange need to be in their company, almost a physical hunger for their presence. Something inside of me had been starved for a long time, and now it was making up for lost time. Every time I looked at them, I felt a shyness and a sense of amazement that anyone – outside of Dubhain, of course – could know me as they did and still take such obvious pleasure in my company.

When I hesitatingly mentioned this feeling to them, Ralph smiled at me knowingly and nodded, explaining to me that they had all felt much the same thing when they first had created the bond between the three of them. The feeling would soon pass as the security of what I was part of became a visceral reality, but till that happened I would crave close contact with them.

"And that's ok," he finished with a smile. "We like hanging out with you, too."

And that seemed to be true, because Sandy and Peter spent most of the next day with me too. Sometimes we just sat and read or listened to music, and for awhile in the afternoon, Sandy took both of us downstairs and played the piano for us. It seemed like he knew every song I could think of to ask him to play, and a whole lot of things I had never heard before. I laughed my ass off when he did a camp rendition of "Girls Just Wanna Have Fun," and nearly cried when I heard the deep, beautiful chords of "Clair de Lune" for the first time.

Things got more serious after Ralph woke up and joined us for dinner, around nine o'clock or so. The meal itself was simple – a green salad, some steamed veggies and quiche. Afterwards, we cleaned up the kitchen and retired to the parlor for a planning session.

The way forward seemed fairly obvious, but it was fraught with danger, that was clear. Somebody was going to die, if Sandy had his way about it. I watched him talk about Braewynn and his exploits and I was amazed that I'd ever thought of him as calm about the whole problem. With my new sense of what was really going on with him, I could feel the depths of his anger and indignation that he did such a good job of hiding on the surface. Further, I could feel the same feelings echoed in both of my other brothers' hearts, and I knew this was something they were deeply committed to doing. It made me anxious, because in spite of their confidence I knew it could turn out very differently than how they were believing it would be. I knew that sometimes the bad guys win.

"So we'll contact the Council of Honor tomorrow morning," Sandy said, "and file our statement of intention. That'll pretty much blow the cover off the whole thing, because they'll contact their opposite number in Unseelie, and they'll inform Braewynn of our intentions."

"And that should take some of the pressure off of us, because Bryon will be beyond Braewynn's reach until the duel is concluded, right?" Ralph commented.

"Um, guys, I hate to be a drag, but what happens if the duel fails? What if Braewynn wins?"

There was a moment of silence, and then Sandy said "Then we will be undone. The clan will be no more, I will be dead, and you will be given to Braewynn to do with as he pleases. It's not an option, you see. We *must* win. And, even though the pimp has a reputation for being a very experienced duelist, I have every confidence that I will win. There is no other acceptable alternative."

"Oh." I digested that in silence for a bit. "All right, I can roll with that." I tried to smile a little, putting on a brave front. I should have known better.

"I know that you're afraid, Bryon," Ralph said softly. "You needn't – you can't – hide anything from us, your brothers. It's only right and natural that you should know some fear and anxiety over this...it means the difference between life and death for all of us. Still, I have seen Sandy in action, and if you thought Lady Elenore was frightening, you haven't seen anything. Sandy is very, very good. We wouldn't be doing this if we didn't think the odds were at least evenly in our favor."

I nodded and tried to tamp down my fear. They really didn't need to be worrying about my fears and anxieties with the upcoming action hanging over their heads.

"So we will all be there when we meet with Braewynn and his crew," Sandy explained. "They will be allowed to bring an equally sized party, by the rules of the Council. I will state our grievance and the terms of our challenge, and Braewynn will have no choice but to accept, because he would lose too much face if he did otherwise. When the actual duel is fought, no one else will be allowed to interfere. But that's the only rule: everything else is fair game. Whatever we each of us bring to the grounds can be used without loss of honor. I have heard that Braewynn prefers to duel with twin rapiers, while I will be using Kaldor." At my blank look, he added "Two handed sword that was a gift a long time ago."

"Ah," I said, and tried to look like I knew anything about swords.

"Don't worry about it," he grinned. "Kaldor and I have won more than our share of duels." And that was where we left it that night, seemingly by common but silent consent not discussing the upcoming duel any further.

The next morning, I awoke early despite the late night the evening before. I felt a sense of energy and animation, a lightness of mood that seemed very at odds with what I knew was scheduled for that day. I thought about it for a moment, and then realized that it wasn't coming from me, but through the clan kin bond. I was catching Sandy's mood, feeling his relief that the wait was over and now some action could be taken on a problem that he had been working on for a very long time. Today he would declare his intentions and have it out in the open, as he preferred it.

After a minimal breakfast, he waited for me to get dressed, telling me to put on the suit I would find hanging in my closet upstairs. I hurried up to the room, curious about what I would find in the closet.

When I opened the door of the armoire – the room, being tucked under the eaves, had no room for a built in closet – I found a charcoal gray suit with lighter gray pinstripes in three pieces, a beautiful and discreetly colorful silk tie, and a pair of black loafers with a pair of black socks stuffed into them. There were braces on the pants, the back of which was leather while the fronts were silk in the same pattern as the tie. On another hanger was a dove gray linen shirt, which picked up the pinstripes in the suit. It was a very beautiful, and very conservative outfit. Not my kind of thing at all, but I gritted my teeth and put it all on. In a gesture of rebellion, I left the top button of the shirt undone and the tie pulled down slightly. All the clothes were perfectly fitted and went on flawlessly. I looked in the cheval glass when I was dressed, and an elegant stranger was looking back at me. His hair was a mess though, so it wasn't a total loss. Long live the revolution!

Back downstairs, Sandy perused me with a critical eye while Peter looked at me with hidden laughter in his smile. I knew he was just relieved it was me in the monkey suit and not him. Sandy gave his approval of the clothes, but pulled me into the downstairs bathroom and crushed my small rebellion with a round brush, a spray bottle and a blow drier. I was soon coifed within an inch of my life, and somehow the top button of my shirt was secured and my tie pulled up. I admit it – I pouted over that one.

Sandy himself was looking very elegant in a cream toned linen suit, tan leather belt and matching shoes. His socks were carefully beige and matched both his shoes and the pale leather vest he wore. His hair was pulled back into a long pony tail and secured with an enameled clasp which bore a strange device that looked almost like what you would see on a knight's shield. When I asked him about it, he said that it was the coat of arms of Agryvaine, the realm ruled by his mother.

"We'll be dealing with people today that place a great deal of emphasis on the importance of tradition, and correct etiquette. They're very, very conservative and hidebound I'm afraid, so every step of the dance we're about to start must be pre-planned and carefully executed. The Council members we'll be talking to will be the ones who decide whether our grievance warrants the issuance of a challenge, so we need to have them on our side right from the start." Sandy glanced over at me, his eyes very serious as he drove Ralph's old volvo wagon out of the driveway and started down the hill towards Broadway. "You will need to say as little as possible, answer only the questions that are put to you, and not volunteer any information. They will be well aware that I left Faerie under a cloud, but I was never officially censured, so it won't be an issue here. My mother has maintained my presence in the rolls of her House, so that will work for us, I think."

I nodded silently, somewhat intimidated by the whole thing. I was going to meet other members of the ruling class of Seelie Court, that was clear.

We rolled down Broadway to Denny, then turned right and down the hill, heading west across town. We were both pretty quiet for awhile. The car didn't have a radio or CD player, so it was just the two of us, and no music. When Denny finally curved around into Leary Way, I broke the silence.

"Where are we going, Sandy?"

He shook himself out of his thoughts and glanced at me. "Ballard. The local portal is there."

"The what?"

"The local Seelie waypoint is in Ballard. It's one of the oldest parts of town, and pretty quiet, and that's two big pluses as far as the powers-that-be are concerned. They don't like nosy neighbors, and they don't like modern."

"Oh."

Sandy cracked a little smile at me. "Don't worry, Bryon. I'll explain as much as I can as we go along. For right now, I need to get us to Ballard in one piece, and this ancient pile of rubbish that Ralph calls a car is making that a little difficult. We'll talk more when we get there, hmm?"

I nodded, noting for the first time the little beads of sweat on his forehead and the rough way that he was driving. It seemed that cars pulling up alongside him on the road made him pretty nervous, and he'd always either pull forward or drop back when it happened. I was mildly amazed – something he wasn't good at! Who knew?

"You know, I could drive on the way back. I'm pretty comfortable behind the wheel." I didn't get an answer for that beyond a distracted frown as the car in the next lane veered slightly toward us and Sandy stepped on the brake to let it move on past. The car behind us honked at him, and Sandy gasped and stepped on the gas, lurching us forward. Without a word I reached over, pulled on the seatbelt and snapped it into place, which earned me a dark look from my companion.

Finally, we turned off of Market street and onto 27th in Ballard. After a couple of blocks, Sandy pulled into an empty parking lot beside a big, worn old building which must have been attractive in its day, but now looked rather dilapidated and nondescript. He relaxed a little as he turned off the ignition.

Sandy sighed in relief. "Thank gods we're here. I truly hate driving, but sometimes it can't be helped. Come on, let's get out and talk for a minute and then we'll do this thing."

The building we were parked in front of had a sign over the front door: Oddfellows Hall 253, with a three link chain symbol beneath the name. I remembered that there was an Oddfellows hall on Capital Hill as well, but I had no idea who they might have been. If Sandy noticed my curiosity, he ignored it.

"All right," he said, "this is it. We're going to go in there and register a complaint and issue a challenge against Braewynn for his treatment of you, going through the official channels. We want this to be as letter perfect as possible, to prevent wiggle room for him to complicate matters, so you need to know what's going on in case something unexpected happens. I don't believe that will happen, but ya never know, right?

"Inside that building, there is a portal to Faerie that will land us in the offices of the Honor Council – they have a longer official name, but that's what it boils down to. They handle all the dueling requests and, with their opposite number in Unseelie court, set up times and places and handle all the small details and arrangements. When we show up there they'll know who we are but they'll ask us for our identities anyway, and I'll present our bona fides. Then they'll ask for the particulars of our complaint, and I'll give them a brief rundown of what happened to you, and what our challenge will consist of. There may be some questions over a challenge to the death, but I have the right and they'll have to agree. Your job will be to stay as quiet as possible and agree when they ask if you bear witness to what I've said, ok?"

I grinned a little. "Keep my mouth shut unless spoken to directly, and then agree. I think I've got it."

Sandy smiled a little wryly. "That's about the truth of it. It's all rigamarole, but it's what we have to get through if we want to get Braewynn off your back and serve a little justice on him at the same time. Don't let these guys intimidate you – they're here to do what we want them to do, but the little power of their position sometimes goes to their heads. No matter what they say, stay serious and focus on our purpose, because all the rest is just posturing."

"That bad, eh?" I was getting a little worried.

"They might try to shake me up a little, but I can handle anything they can throw at me. I've dealt with these kinds of people for a long time. I managed to live through the people at DMV, and this'll be a cakewalk compared to that."

"Right. Let's do it then."

"Let's."

With that, Sandy turned and headed toward the rusty, worn door in the front of the brick building, with me following a pace behind.

(9)

The door was locked, of course. Sandy sighed and cursed under his breath, then laid his hand on the door just above the knob and murmured about three words. When he tried the handle again, the door opened easily, and he led the way into the dark foyer of the building.

Inside, I looked around but it looked like any old, abandoned building except for the lack of tagging and other vandalism. When the door closed, the hall went completely dark for a moment, and then a muted light bloomed around us from a small globe that Sandy held in one hand. Looking across the room, I could just make out two doors on the opposite wall, one on each side of a staircase that led up to the second floor, its upper reaches lost in shadow.

Sandy smiled at me and commented, "All very cloak and dagger, isn't it? Still, a portal to Faerie isn't something you can put in Westlake Mall with a big sign over it, right? Let's head up the stairs – the door we want is up there." He started for the stairs, and then paused. "Wait, there's one other thing I need to do. All the proceedings in the Honor Council are conducted in High Elvish – do you speak it?"

"No, never got around to learning that," I said. "Kind of busy, y'know?"

"Yeah. Well, you're going to need to know what's going on, and they might be offended if you don't know the language; I can give you a gift of tongues, if you want. I think it's the easiest solution, unless you want to spend a few decades learning the language first."

I grinned at him and shook my head. "Naw, think I'll pass on that. So what do we need to do?"

"Just hold still a moment, and I'll do it now." With that, he left the globe of light hanging in the air and put one hand on each side of my head, over my ears. He said a few words in a language I didn't know, and I felt a tingle in each ear and at the back of my throat. He pulled his hands away and spoke to me again.

"All right, can you understand what I'm saying?" It sounded like he was speaking english, but at the same time I could hear an echo of a totally foreign language beneath his words.

I nodded, and I could tell my eyes were wide open. He laughed a little at my expression and patted me on the shoulder. "I put a three day limit on it, so after three days you won't understand or speak the language anymore. I can go back in later and make it permanent if you want, but it takes a lot more time. This should work for now." With that, he turned back to the stairs and started up, the little light globe bobbing along in his wake and me right on his heels.

The second floor of the building was equally as dark and dilapidated as the first floor. I followed Sandy down a wide hall, until he stopped in front of a closed door on the right.

"All right, this is it. When we walk through this door, we'll be in the chambers of the Honor Council. Remember your instructions?" He smiled when I nodded. "Good. Let's get this done, then." With that, he grasped the doorknob, opened the door and led the way into the room beyond.

There wasn't any transition. One moment we were in an abandoned, shabby hallway, and the next we were in a large, open, and richly appointed hall. There weren't any walls, just a series of pillars and arches supporting a roof over a stone floor. It seemed to all be built of milky quartz – sort of translucent in places, and solid in others. A series of guards stood in place near the arches, four on each side, all dressed in some kind of uniform: long tunics, tight breeks and mail shirts, with a tabard belted at the waist. Each tabard was black with silver trim, and had a picture of a bird and a star on the chest. They each had a sword and dagger in scabbards at their sides, and a small shield slung across their backs. A few others – all Lios Alfar from what I could see – walked back and forth carrying papers and scrolls, occasionally pausing to confer with each other or with the two elves who sat behind a pair of desks at the far end of the hall. All this activity stopped when we showed up, though. For a moment they all just looked at us, and then slowly went on about their business.

All this I saw in the first seconds, and then my attention was drawn to the two who sat behind the twin desks. Another elf who had been standing between the desks and carried a long staff with a crystal on the head of it stepped forward and called out to us, "Approach, strangers. Make known your names, and state your business with the Council."

Sandy didn't answer, but strode forward with confidence while I followed him with a lot less. I noticed in passing that he had dropped his human glamour and I felt even more gauche as the only human-looking person in the room.

When we stood in front of the twin desks, Sandy bowed deeply to both of those who sat at them, and then rose back to his feet and I could feel him bracing himself.

"I am hight Sandellifer, knight-champion of Dusksong, member in good standing of the Order of the Roseate Blade and heir-apparent to the realm of Agryvaine. I am come to exercise my right of challenge on behalf of this, my clan brother. One there is who has wronged and dishonored him, and I seek to set that wrong to rights, proving the verity of our claim on his body." He'd said the whole thing in one breath, and it had the sound of ritual to it. I wondered how many versions of those same words had been spoken in this hall over the many years.

Though Sandy had remained calm as he had spoken, there was nothing calm about the ringing intensity in his voice, and all activity in the hall had stopped as he declared his intentions. Every eye in the place was focused on him, and there was a moment of silence.

Finally the silence was broken by one of the men behind the two desks at the front of the room. His voice had the same smooth cadences as Sandy's when he spoke in the High Elven tongue, but with a hint of lazy drawl.

"So, Sandellifer ap Agryvaine, you return when once again your muddied honor is called into question. Before last you disappeared, your name was called into question here quite frequently, and by many of good and solid repute. I recall no answer from you to any of it but the acceptance of those challenges. Why should we hear you now?"

"Because despite your questioning, you know that my honor is now, and has ever been, intact. Others have called it into question, and those questions have been dealt with on the field of honorable combat. They required no more answer than that, and

131

well you know it, Lord Torrel." Though Sandy's voice remained calm, I could feel a hint of heat coming over the clan bond. I hoped it was going ok, but it honestly didn't look very good.

Than I did a double take as the challenging lord smiled a little returned to his seat. The elf standing between the desks stepped forward a little.

"My lords, one approaches who requests an audience with Your Graces, one who would present a grievance against his honor. Will you hear his case?"

Lord Torell, who had spoken to Sandy before, leaned forward and looked at us very hard before he spoke. He was a tall, slim man, with golden blonde hair pulled back tightly in a ponytail at the back. His whole demeanor was one of relaxed arrogance, but his blue eyes shone with lively curiosity.

"Yes, I think we will, Madoc. I have a feeling this morning is going to get a lot more interesting before it's over, eh Daindraen?" He looked sharply over at his opposite number at the other desk.

The elf seated there was, in many ways, the opposite of his counterpart. Where Torell was tall and golden, Daindraen was short, heavy and thick. His hair was dark, and cut very short on the sides and only slightly longer on top. His skin, though fair as any Lios Alfar's, showed the effects of time spent under a hot sun and whipping winds – a faint bronzing of his face and hands, all that showed from beneath his long, ceremonial robes. Despite the elaborate robes, he looked hard and tough, like someone who I definitely would not have wanted to meet in a dark alley.

I happened to be looking at Sandy's face when the second Lord's name was mentioned, and I saw his control break for the only time in the whole ordeal. For just a second, he looked absolutely incredulous, and then his guard snapped up tight and he was again impassive, waiting for their response.

Unlike the first Lord, this elf's voice was deep and rough. "We shall see, shan't we, Torell? Bring them forward, Madoc. Who is that puppy dogging Sandellifer's heels?"

Well, this certainly wasn't going much like Sandy had warned me it might. These two were almost casual – what the hell? I almost startled when I felt Sandy's hand on my back, pushing me forward a little.

"My lords, I would introduce to you my squire Bryon, a sealed member of the Clan of the Red Circle. It is he to whom indignity and dishonor has been offered."

"Another stray, eh Sandellifer? By my hope of the Summer Lands, before you're done you'll have taken in every sad and displaced pup in the human lands. So what happened to this one?" Torell's voice was a slow and amused drawl.

I felt Sandy stiffen a little next to me. "Bryon is a brother of strength and spirit, and a valuable addition to the well being of our clan." His voice was crisp, though restrained.

"Don't get offended, young knight. No insult is intended, I'm sure. No doubt he's a lion, though he looks but a pup. You have a way of picking the best even as you're rescuing, as any who have watched you know."

Sandy inclined his head a bit, and murmured "My thanks, my lord." Then he straightened and looked directly at the two of them. "I request the honor of privy council, my lords. I would not have this tale bandied about as common gossip." I saw a quick look of startlement on Torell's face, then it was back to the smooth, glib mask he had worn up to that point. Daindraen glanced over at his companion councillor and then nodded abruptly and stood.

"Come on, then," he rumbled. "We'll use the ready room behind us."

Torell looked amused for a moment as he watched Madoc look about in surprise, then hurry across the floor to precede the burly lord to a door in the wall behind the desks. With almost undignified haste, the seneschal of the Honor Council whipped open the door and stepped aside as Daindraen brushed past him. With a graceful economy of movement, the second lord stood and waved us forward, and we followed him back to and through the door.

As the door closed behind us, I saw that Daindraen was already seated on a large wingback chair, with his booted feet up on an ottoman. He looked at us silently, but somehow I caught an almost amused look on his grim face.

"Have a seat, lads. There's wine on the sideboard, yonder – help yourselves, if you'd like. I think we can dispense with the claptrap of the Honor Council, don't you? I'm Torell, and that's Daindraen. Now, let's get down to cases. What brings you here today?" Torell stepped over to a nearby sofa and sat down on the edge of the seat, leaning forward and obviously ready to listen.

I felt a little flash of surprise through the clan bond, but Sandy's face remained calm. He waved me to a seat on a sofa next to Daindraen and sat himself next to me.

"Well m'lords, it's a bit of a tale. I hope you'll indulge the telling."

"Out with it, boy. We've nothing but time here, after getting roped into Council duty. Let's hear what has passed." Daindraen's face was hard and intent, his eyes cool but curious.

And so, Sandy told the tale. He kept it simple and straightforward, and unflinchingly honest. The first time Braewynn's name came up, I saw Torrel shift in his seat a little, but that was the only indication that either of them knew who he was. Sandy also, to my surprise, explained the intention of the Clan to curtail the Drow's trade in human children, but almost as a sidenote. Not a lot was said on the subject, but I noticed a narrowing of Torrel's eyes, and Daindraen's face became, somehow, more stonily hard than ever.

As Sandy finished, there was a moment of silence as the two of them thought about what they had heard. I could feel both of them looking at me.

"So, young Pooka, you have agreed to allow Sandy to act in your stead in this action, not so?" Torell questioned.

"Yes, m'lord," I murmured, my eyes downcast.

"And it is your wish, Sandellifer, that this duel be to the death, yes? I'm not sure that will fly, you know – the affront is a little weak for that provision. It may well be that Braewynn will be given the option of accepting that part or no. Other than that, I see no reason not to go forward with this, eh Torrel? Clearly intent to harm and suborning of will were present, and I think we can add several other offenses to the list as well. There may be some quibbling about the timing – it happened before Bryon was your clan mate – but I think we can get this done." Daindraen's face was alight, and he had a tight smile on his lips.

"Don't do half measures, do you, Sandellifer? Braewynn is a big fish over there – Duke of Athelon now days, as I recall. Oh yes, this is going to set the hawk among the hens." Torrel was almost rubbing his hands together in anticipation.

Sandy had a little smile on his face. "I'm so glad we could provide a small distraction in an otherwise long and dull day, m'lords," he murmured.

"You have no idea, boy. I was trying to decide if I could get away with signing orders when you two arrived," Daindraen replied. "We both were twiddling our thumbs and praying the day would fly by. I've got too much to do to be sitting in an empty hall and wasting time with this dandy." He waved at Torrel with a smile.

"And this one has the eloquence of a marble monument. All morning and naught but three words out of him the whole time." As he spoke, Torrel rose from his seat and crossed to the sideboard, pouring himself a glass of wine. He looked inquiringly at Daindraen, who nodded, and he poured a second goblet for the taciturn lord. Sandy demurred when Torrel made the same offer to us.

"Well then, we'll write this up and present it to the Unseelie, if that's all the details. Should be fun to watch them react, if naught else. Hasn't been a challenge at this level for quite some time, I believe."

"Are we done here, then? Go on home, lads, and we'll contact you when we have a response. Look for a courier on the third day, I would think. The scribes here will write it all up properly, and the courier should have the time, date and place when you see him, after a little to-and-fro-ing," Daindraen said. "It's been a pleasure meeting both you and your clan brother, young Sandellifer. My regards to your mother when next you see her, eh?" Daindraen stood, and instead of the bow or head nod I would have expected, he stepped forward and clasped Sandy's forearm in a gesture of respect between warriors. Sandy was clearly startled, but returned the gesture with sincerity, adding a bow of the head and a fist against his chest, over his heart. Torrel also stood and nodded his head to both of us and then slipped from the room, followed by Daindraen, leaving us alone in the small room.

When they'd gone, I turned to Sandy. "I thought you said this was going to be an exercise in protocol. What the hell just happened?"

Sandy just shook his head. "We have been more lucky and honored than we had any right to expect, Bryon. Those two are...well, they're so far beyond the need for etiquette, I don't think I can even explain. We've just been in the presence of two of the greatest warrors ever to come out of Seelie. Torrel is the premiere duelist in the entire court, acting as the Queen's own champion. Daindraen is Lord Commander of all Seelie's military, second only to the King in power. I'd never seen him before, and I nearly fainted when I heard his name out there."

"Wow, heavy hitters eh?"

"The heaviest. To go higher, we'd have needed the King and Queen sitting behind those desks.In fact, they are the only two who don't take a turn working in the Honor Hall. It's all done by lottery, so it's incredible that we got both of them on the same day." Sandy shook his head in amazement. "It will speak well for us that our claim will be presented by two such as they, and since they will also be present at the actual duel, it will ensure honor is maintained there as well. With those two in attendance, the eyes of the all the court will be on us."

"Time to go home and wait, I guess. Didn't they say three days till we'd know? Damn, this is going to be a rough three days," I said.

So, it was back out through the abandoned building and into the old Volvo, which failed to start despite a stream of abuse directed at it by Sandy while I tried to hide a smirk. Luckily, I found a can of fast start spray in the trunk, and a few squirts into the carburetor while Sandy cranked the engine and continued to cuss the car got it started. I mentioned that I wasn't sure which had actually gotten it started – the spray or his invective. He glared at me and drove jerkily out of the parking lot, headed home.

(10)

The next three days were quiet. I stayed at home, getting up late and spending much of the nights up with Ralph. I also spent a lot of time in my head with Dubhain, and I finally found out what all his cryptic comments were about, the ones about us being one.

Since there wasn't a ready source of water in the manse, as my clan brothers called the house, I had taken to spending the afternoons in my head with Dubhain, since both Peter and Sandy were often busy with their own concerns at that time of day. I would get up late, eat lunch with them and head back to bed to spend some time with my horse brother, appearing on the little, winding trail to find him there and waiting for me. I could tell there was something he wanted to talk to me about, but he seemed strangely shy about it – something I was not used to from him. There had never been anything we couldn't talk about before, and it made me a little nervous.

So finally, I just asked him: "Dubhain, what is it? You can talk to me, you know. Gods know, we've talked about everything up to this point, including several things I would just as soon have not talked about. So, what's going on?"

"I would have waited till after the duel to talk about this, Bryon. I know that you have much on your mind, and I would not have burdened you with it, but perhaps now is a good time after all, being that we are waiting on the pleasure of others."

As he had been speaking, he had walked across the clearing toward me and now stood next to me. He paused and lipped at my hair a moment, and rubbed his head against my chest, an expression of affection that he used but rarely. I pulled his head over beside mine and lay my cheek against the rough hair of his jaw and put my arms around his neck, and we stood like that a long moment before he went on.

"I know the desire of your heart, Bryon, and the confusion of your mind when you come to see me. I know that you long for the carefree life that you perceive my existence to be, and my heart has, for long and long, ached with the pain of your life amongst the humans. When I think of what has passed, and how you were hurt and abused, I would kill them all if I could."

"I know, Dubhain, and I'm sorry. I couldn't think of anything else to do..."

"Hush, little brother. I would not bring you grief. That is the music of the past, and I think we needn't go back to it. There is a thing we must talk about, which touches on our life before but is not of it, do you see?"

I was confused, but stood there silently with my arms still around his neck, holding his face next to mine and just waited for him to continue.

"Events have conspired to bring us to a place of companionship, of closeness and intimacy with these others, our clan brothers. But we cannot bring all that we can be to this place unless we have become the fullness of ourselves, and I would tell you that we have not. We live a fractured and sundered life, brother, and it should not be. This separated life is unnatural to us, and it must be mended if we would live as we are intended to be."

"What do you mean, Dubhain? I don't get it. I thought you were happy with me."

"I love you Bryon, and no other. This is as it has always been, and will never change. But this place, this home I have created in your mind, it should not be necessary. We should be one, brother, not two living in one mind. I know not how to make it so, but there is a longing in my heart that speaks to me, telling me that we can be more."

I sat down and wrapped my arms around my chest, felt his warm, whiskery chin on the top of my head and thought about what he had said.

If I said I'd never felt what he was talking about, I'd be a liar. I'd denied it, put down the vague discontent I'd always felt about myself as my feelings about what I did with those others, the tricks. When it stayed with me after that was over, I'd passed it off as lingering guilt, though I'd never really felt guilty about all of that. It was just something I had to do to get by, and even at the time I had known that it didn't really touch who I was, somehow.

Now, Dubhain's comments had opened new possibilities. When we'd entered the clan bond, a part of us I'd never even known was empty became full. Were there other parts of us I didn't know about? Perhaps someplace in us where we became one being, without the sundering that he spoke of? What would that be like? I felt an odd mixture of fear and hope as I thought of it. Would I lose myself – the part that was Bryon – in such a blending? Who would we be after something like that?

I'd been thinking all of this while still open to Dubhain, and he'd heard all of it. His presence was calming, a gentle warmth against the chill of my doubts and fears.

"Do not be afraid, brother. This is no rebellion, no attempt at dominion. Nothing will be lost, only much gained when we have reached this state. Only, like you, I do not know how to reach it. I have studied the problem from many angles, and I see no place to begin, for I don't really know what it is that I seek. I feel the possibility, and I know that it is what awaits us, yet I see no path ahead of us. Perhaps we must be shown – I do not know."

We didn't say a lot more about it at that point, but that conversation stayed with me... at least until other, more immediate concerns came into play.

It was mid evening when the knock we'd all been waiting for sounded on our front door. Ralph had just gotten up, and we were all sitting in the parlor and making small talk, discussing our day and catching up with each other when the knocker banged. It was almost comical the way we all stopped and looked at each other, as if to say 'Well, this is it.' Peter got up and headed out to answer the door, and the rest of us sat in silence and waited for his return.

When he came back, he had someone with him – a young elf, but standing nearly as tall as Peter. His skin was Lios Alfar pale, but his hair was so black it had a blue sheen in the soft light of the lamps in the parlor. He was dressed head to toe in bike messenger spandex, had a bike helmet under his arm, and a mail bag slung across from his left shoulder to his right hip, complete with a handheld radio clipped to the strap. Despite his appearance and the english that he spoke, he was oddly formal.

"I am Jorleon, of the Royal courier service. I seek Sir Sandellifer, formerly of Agryvaine. Is that one present?"

"I am Sandellifer, good courier. You honor our home with your presence. Have you a message for me?"

"If you are Sandellifer, than I do indeed. One moment, please." With that, the courier straightened even more than previously and turned his eyes to the far wall of the room. When he spoke again, his voice was no longer his own, but that of Lord Torrel, whom I had met at the Honor Hall. The lord's voice was distinctive, with a lilting accent when speaking english and still possessing the slightly lazy drawl.

"Hello and good evening to all the members of the clan of the Red Circle. Word has returned from the Unseelie Honor Council, and here is the way of it. First, your challenge is accepted. Second, your mortal stipulation is also accepted, so the duel will be to death. Third, Braewynn has added a stipulation – as is his right, as the challenged – that should he win, he will attach all your holdings, and your squire, Bryon, will be turned over to him as his ward, to do with as he sees fit. Additionally, the rest of your clan kin will be exiled to a place of his choosing, never to return. These are his terms, and he has stated they are non-negotiable.

"This raises the bar a good bit, Sandellifer, but I know that you were aware of the risks going into this, so I will not insult you by asking if you are steadfast in your determination. As a formality, we need an answer sent back to us with young Jorleon here, but I think I already know what it will be. I will await your answer, and then proceed." There was a pause, and I thought the courier was finished until the voice started again, but only briefly.

"On a more personal note, I wish you all the best in this effort, Sandellifer – for the sake of your mother, whom I hold to be a close and dear friend, for the sake of your small clan, which I hold as an inspiration in endurance and good will, and for the sake of the children whom that scorpion has corrupted. Oh, and

Daindraen says 'Make us proud, boy!' as well. I'll wait for your answer."

With that, Jorleon fell silent, and then seemed to regain his sense of self, looking at us expectantly.

"I thank you again, Jorleon, for your excellent service. I will be sending a message back to Lords Torrel and Daindraen, if you will be kind enough to wait. Perhaps you'd like a bit of refreshment?

Jorleon bowed slightly at the waist, and spoke calmly. "No, but thanks, good Sir. I was told to expect a reply, and I am under no pressure of time or place, so I will await your pleasure with good will. If I might be seated while I wait?"

"By all means, Jorleon, and forgive my lack of courtesy in not offering such immediately. Yon fire is warm and the chair comfortable, so please be at your ease while my brothers and I parley and compose a reply."

"Very well. Please do not hurry your reply on my account, m'lord. I am at your disposal."

With that, Sandy bowed to the courier, and the four of us retreated to the kitchen for a quick talk.

"Well, there you have it: every bit as bad as we thought it would be. The bastard will take it all if I lose."

"We knew that's how it would be going into this, Sandy. I didn't hear anything surprising in that message, except perhaps the personal note at the end. That's not normal, is it?" Ralph's voice was quiet and calm.

"No, that was a surprise to me too, actually. This could turn into something a lot bigger than we thought it would be. With

Torrel and Daindraen involved, you can be sure the King and Queen know and are following this. I wouldn't be surprised if there was a bit of an audience at the actual event."

I listened to all this, appalled at their casual attitudes. They acted like they were discussing whether to go to the county fair or not, while everything they had ever worked for was at risk.

"What is wrong with you two? This could be the end of everything, and you two are acting as though none of it matters!"

Sandy shot me a sidelong look, and actually smiled. Ralph at least took me seriously, and explained.

"It doesn't matter at this point, Bryon. The die is cast, and nothing can take back the decision to issue the challenge in the first place. I assure you that Peter and I would just as soon not be exiled to a place of Braewynn's choosing, and we'd all prefer to continue to live out our lives in this lovely home, but now there is only waiting and then victory. What good would wailing and beating of the breast do now? None, I assure you. No, this has been coming for a very long time, and we have had much time to study the seriousness of what we proposed."

I felt Peter's big paw land on my shoulder. "I think you need a sandwich, Bryon. Being hungry always makes me tense. Might do you good." I flashed him a warm smile – of all my brothers, Peter was the kindest and most concerned. Though a sandwich seemed woefully inadequate in the face of what I had just heard in the parlor, I knew he was doing what he could to set me at ease. I nodded a little, and he hurried to the refrigerator and started taking out cold cuts and all the fixings for two of his enormous sandwich specials.

While Peter fussed over our small – by his standards, anyway – meal, Sandy outlined his intention to agree to all of Braewynn's stipulations, but that he would be adding further conditions of his own: when he won, he would be given all of the Pimp's material possessions in the human realms; all of the commercial ventures he was associated with here would be terminated immediately; and any 'talent' involved in his moviemaking and sales efforts were to be unharmed and turned over to the Clan of the Red Circle.

"We don't know how many children could be involved, nor how damaged and traumatized they might be, so I'm going to ask my mother to take them in if there is more than just a couple. I'm pretty sure it won't be a problem – though she doesn't like anyone to notice, she likes having children around, and her manor house in Agryvaine is set up for this a lot better than the manse. All right then, is there anything else?" He paused and looked at all of us. "No? Let's get back in there and send our reply then."

Peter and I left our sandwiches waiting on the counter, and all four of us trooped back into the parlor, where Jorleon sat in the over-stuffed wingback chair in front of the tiny fireplace, his feet up on a hassock. Hearing the door open, he rose to his feet and looked at Sandy expectantly.

"You have a message to be sent?"

"Aye, by your leave, I would have you take a message to Lords Torrel and Daindraen."

"Very good. If you will speak it clearly and slowly, in the voice and words that you would have them hear, I shall endeavor to convey it to them."

"Very well, then. Beginning now: My Lords Torrel and Daindraen, hail! My deepest appreciation and respect are yours for the work that you both have done on my behalf and on behalf of the Clan of the Red Circle. We are indebted to you both, and shall strive mightily if, and when, you find a need for our services in whatever matter you see fit. We are yours to command.

"Regarding the matter at hand, my brothers and I accept the stipulations laid upon our challenge and defiance of Braewynn of Athelon, and we would add some stipulations of our own, as is our right. When the victory is ours, we will assume ownership of all his lands and holdings in the human realms, retroactive to the date of the original insult that precipitated this event. Further, each, any, every and all of his commercial ventures shall be terminated – not just in his involvement, but disbanded entirely. Lastly, the Clan of the Red Circle will be given possession of any children currently under his owernership, and all records of the sale of any and all children up to this point, in all of his ventures. These terms are absolute and non-negotiable.

"We await, with great anticipation, your message informing us of the time and place where this series of unfortunate events will be concluded. Again, both my brothers and I thank you for all that you have done for us in this matter."

There was a long pause, and then Jorleon smiled and nodded. "As well you know, I will deliver this message without fail, Sandellifer. Now, I have further messages to deliver. The first is for you, good sir. It is addressed for your ears only, though the sender adds that your clan brothers may hear it, at your discretion."

"I have no secrets from my brothers. If you will deliver the message, I will hear it."

The courier smiled and nodded. "A moment then." His eyes once again lost focus and he began to speak, this time in the voice that I remembered from my encounter in the garden: the cool, clear voice of Lady Elenore.

"Word of your doings have arrived at my demesne, my son, and I am proud of you, as ever. I am aware that you are cognizant of the manner of foe that you will face, but I would remonstrate on one point: Unseelie honor is not the honor of Seelie. Their honor lies in outcomes, not in process. When battling such a foe, there must be no quarter granted, no allowance for weakness, and no concern for dishonorable battle tactics. You must carry in your mind the determination to crush your foe in any way that you may, and be wary for tactics from him that would be beyond the pale, did you face a Seelie opponent.

"I will strive to be present at the event, and it is my hope that you would see fit to carry the favor of the Duchess of Agryvaine into battle with you. Know that my best wishes and care are with you at all times, and my greetings to all your clan brothers as well."

Jorleon again fell silent, and his eyes refocused before he turned to me. "You are called Bryon, no? If so, then my last message is for you, and it is of the same origin as the last." With hardly a pause, he spoke again in Lady Elenore's voice.

"It is well that you have joined with my son and his brothers in clan kinship, young Bryon. I am well pleased that you have avoided your foe's clutches thus far, and I hope that this will continue to be the case. Should you need refuge at any time forget not Agryvaine, for you shall find welcome here. Lords of the Summerlands forbid, but should darkness fall upon your cause, remember the boon you have accepted, brother to my son, and all may yet be well."

Though she wasn't in the room, I nodded soberly. I was a little relieved that we had a fall-back position, even though I was trying as hard as I could to be positive about the outcome of this whole debacle. The calm in Elenore's voice was something I really needed just about then.

A day later, Jorleon showed up again, this time carrying confirmation that the lords had received our answer, and giving us the details of time and place: Two days hence at 11pm, an abandoned cow pasture 25 miles to the south, near Enumclaw, would see the end of this whole affair.

(11)

The next two days were surprisingly uneventful. Life at the Manse went on just about the same way it did before. One night we had a couple of kids over for dinner with us – a girl and a boy who lived on the streets in the University district most of the time, but who stopped by a couple times a week for a meal and sometimes more often in the winter, when the weather was just a little too cold for sleeping outdoors. They were good kids, but there was a look of desperation in their eyes that I didn't like, and I decided to keep close tabs on their whereabouts while they were in the house. When you have nothing but the clothes on your back and whatever you can carry with you, personal ethics become a luxury you can't afford. I wouldn't have been surprised if they had pocketed a few items to take with them.

Sure enough, when they'd left and I was doing a quick inventory to make sure they hadn't left with anything, I noticed that a small silver vase had gone missing, and so had a little statuette of some kind of egyptian god that had been sitting on a side table in the parlor.

"Sandy, wasn't there a silver vase sitting over there on the corner in the kitchen? And what about that little egyptian thing in the parlor? Did those two take them?"

"Yeah, they did. They'll be able to sell 'em for a few dollars and eat for a couple days."

"You knew about it? Why didn't you stop them?"

"But that's what we bought them for, Bryon. We've offered those two money before, and they wouldn't accept any. So now when they come over, they know that there are two items – always in the same places – that they can take. Everything else is spelled to return to the house as quickly as possible, you see, and it didn't take them long to figure it all out. Now they just take the two items to hold them over till their next meal here, and no one says a word about it."

I stared at him for a moment, and then just shook my head. "But how do you know that they won't bring their friends and break... oh."

"Yeah. Wards work pretty well against burglars, too."

The following day, our last before the challenge date, was spent with all of us in the house and just relaxing together. Sandy disappeared for a couple of hours around mid day as he often did, explaining that he was off to the gym. I asked if I could go with him but he gently refused, explaining that we would need to buy a membership for me before I could go. I thought that was odd, since most gyms will sell a membership right on the spot.

After Sandy was gone, Peter explained. Sandy wasn't going to a gym per se, but to an arms trainer – a master swordsman who lived in the Midlands and trained students from both Seelie and Unseelie courts. There wasn't much left that he could teach Sandy, Peter continued, but they sparred a lot together and Sandy taught some of his entry level students. I thought about that for a while, and decided that I might like to go with him sometime, for real. It was time for me to learn to defend myself, if we all survived beyond the next day.

I stayed up late with Ralph, drinking coffee and talking. When he first got up, all four of us went out to Mike's and had breakfast, which was a little odd since it was ten o'clock at night, but no one commented. We came home after and Sandy went into the kitchen and put on the coffee pot, and we all sat around and talked for hours. I already knew the story of how Ralph and Sandy had met Peter, but they told the story again from each of their perspectives and it felt good to hear the clan's history and know that I was a piece of that history now, that we were making the history of our clan even now, right there in the parlor of the Manse. We talked about how the clan would slowly grow as we found others in need and with the qualifications to join, and it was comforting to know that we were all planning for life beyond the duel, because it made the possibility of victory that much more real.

At 8 am, Ralph and I both went to bed, and I didn't get up till 4 pm, and just like that it was the day of the duel. By midnight tonight, the fate of the Clan of the Red Circle would be decided. Sandy had been up since 11 am and gone for a short run, followed by a big meal of pasta for carbo loading. It was interesting to watch him prepare. He spent several hours in the basement staring at a candle and breathing slowly; after a couple of hours I heard the piano from down there, and I knew it was ok to go down and listen. Sandy didn't seem to even notice me when I crept into the room and just kept on playing, his hands flashing over the keyboard and creating the most amazing music. I knew, just by listening, that this wasn't the music of human history, but of elven work. The piece was long and complicated, with strange twists and turnings that I would never have expected but which somehow fit perfectly. I sat on a big recliner, put my head back and retreated inside, ending up on a dry spot in Dubhain's bog. My horse brother had lain down, his legs folded beneath him, I lay on my back with my head resting against his side, and we listened to the beauty that Sandy was making on the piano together.

I came back up when I heard a voice in the room that I had not expected to hear: Elenore's cool voice.

"It has been a long time since I heard that piece, son, and never on such an instrument. You play it well."

I didn't budge, pretending to still be down inside. The music stopped and I heard Sandy move about a little.

"Mother, you came. I wondered if you would."

"Fool of a boy, of course I came. How could I stay away?"

I cracked my eyes open just the tiniest bit, and there she was, as beautiful and elegant as I remembered her from the garden. My heart sped up a little when I saw her – yes, I had a little crush on Sandy's mother, but I also knew that there wasn't a male on the planet who wouldn't have – she was that beautiful.

With a slight smile, she turned to where I was lying back on the recliner. "It is good to see you again, Bryon. You look well. It is clear that you have prospered since joining my son's clan, and that is much to the good."

Busted. I sat up and slid forward, going to one knee in front of her. "M'lady, welcome to the Manse. It is both a pleasure and an honor to see you again."

I was rewarded with a light laugh from her. "Why, young Bryon, your manners have improved remarkably. You have been paying attention, haven't you? I approve. For that, you shall escort me upstairs to inspect this home that you have all made for yourselves."

She held out her hand, and I jumped up to stand beside her and offer her my arm. When I dared to look at her face – just a glance, you understand, because I was still plenty intimidated by her – there was a look of light amusement there, and also of kindness. Following Sandy, we walked up the stairs to the main floor.

Ralph was in his office, working on some accounts when we arrived at his door. The look on his face when he saw who I was escorting was priceless – a moment of shock before he gathered himself and stood, then bowed deeply.

"Lady of Agryvaine, welcome. You honor us deeply. I apologize for my dishabille, but this is most unexpected." Somehow, in spite of his sweats and tee shirt, he radiated dignity.

"When one visits unannounced, one cannot expect a prepared host. It is a pleasure to finally meet you, Ralph the Scholar. I have heard much of you from my son. Perhaps one day, after the current business is done, we can spend a little time together telling tales from the history of my race, as I have heard that you have an interest in such things."

"It would be a great pleasure, m'lady. I look forward to the day. Bryon, why don't you show the Lady to the parlor, and we'll join you there in a moment. I think we have some wine that might be just about right for this moment, and I need to collect Peter. I'll be just a moment."

At that moment, Peter came tromping down the stairs. He was humming tunelessly to himself, and if Ralph's reaction to seeing Lady Elenore had been amusing, Peter's reaction was almost frightening. He stopped dead in his tracks, and then without a word flung himself to both knees and pressed his forehead to the floor at her feet. And stayed there, obviously not intending to move until given permission.

I think we all just kind of stared at him for a moment. I was shocked, and even Sandy and Ralph seemed a little nonplussed. But Lady Elenore didn't even act surprised.

She bent at the waist and laid a hand on his shoulder, not drawing back when he cringed from her touch just a little. Her voice was soft and gentle. "Rise, Peter the Strong. Such obeisance is not needful to me. You are the brother of my son, and as such nearly a son to me in your own right. Come, stand and greet me."

Peter was shaking, trembling in every limb as he stood slowly, and he wouldn't look Elenore in the face, keeping his eyes on the floor. The Lady wasn't having any of that, though. She gently placed two fingers under his chin and raised his face till he looked her directly in the eye.

"We are not enemies, you and I," she chided him gently. "We are allies and more, bound together by the regard that we hold in common for my son. There is no need for fear. I am a simple guest in your home." Turning back to me, she continued in a brisk tone, "Now then, young Bryon, Ralph spoke of a parlor. Perhaps you could show me?"

And so I showed her through the french doors and into the parlor. Though it was still summer, a small fire crackled and popped in the grate of the fireplace, and a couple of lamps were lit, casting a soft yellow light over the room. I seated the Lady on one of the small sofas, and took a place in a nearby chair. Peter sat across the room on the big, overstuffed wingback, and in just a moment we were joined by Ralph and Sandy, with Ralph carrying an opened bottle of wine and Sandy enough red wine glasses for all of us.

"I would appreciate your opinion of this vintage, Lady Elenore. I think you'll find it a bit different from the wines of Faerie." Ralph poured a small bit into goblet for the Lady, and then watched in anticipation as she sipped delicately at the dark red wine.

As she rolled the wine around in her mouth, Elenore's eyes seemed to open just a bit wider.

"This is excellent, Ralph. A bit less smooth than I am used to, but complex and full-bodied. My husband made such wines many years ago…it brings back many memories for me." Without a word, Ralph leaned in and filled her goblet to the halfway mark, then poured a like amount in each glass for us.

Raising his glass, Ralph said, "Here is to the health of our guest, and to the honor done to our clan by the grace of her presence."

When we'd all sipped a bit, Elenore stood. Raising her glass just a little, she returned Ralph's toast with one of her own.

"The blessings of the Sidhe are on this house, and all who dwell in it. Good fortune and prosperity follow you all the days of your lives, and at their end, may you all find a place in the Summerlands."

When she had returned to her seat and we'd all sipped a bit more wine, Elenore delicately cleared her throat and looked over at Sandy.

"I have said that I would wish to send the favor of the Duchess of Agryvaine into battle with you, my son, and so I have brought with me a thing that might be of use to you in the upcoming trial." Reaching into the deep sleeve of her sky blue gown, she pulled out a sheathed dagger and laid it on the coffee table in front of her. "Perhaps you recognize it?"

"Ysendin!" Sandy's voice was hushed, and he looked at the jeweled dagger with awe in his eyes. "But mother, it is one of the great treasures of our house!"

"Not just a great treasure, but a very fine tool. Better it go into battle with you than gather dust in the vaults at Agryvaine."

"If I might ask, what is it?" Ralph was leaning forward in his chair and staring avidly at the dagger.

"It was given to my mother's mother by a great king," Elenore answered. "Forged in some forgotten time, it has a great virtue of healing on it, and will heal wounds taken in battle even as they occur. In addition, it lends its bearer greater strength and agility, so that one may avoid such wounds. It has been in our family's possession for many long years, and now it passes to my son's hand. Bear it well, Sandellifer."

"I shall seek to be worthy of this great gift, mother. I thank you for it with all my heart."

"Very well. I have one other bit of news to impart, and a greeting to give from a long time friend of yours."

"Oh? A long time friend, you say? I do not have any such from the realms of faerie, as I recall."

Elenore smiled. "But you do, though you know it not. I bear greetings and best wishes for your victory from one named Alreid, a scholar in the house of Agryvaine."

"Alreid? By my hope! Mother, what are you up to? How did this come to pass?"

"Well, it seems that after you left, your Alreid fell prey to great grief and shame over his role in the deception that led to your departure. He was ever a delicate creature, sensitive and tender of heart, as you know. Eventually it became too much for him, and he confessed all to his father, the Duke of Myrandis. That worthy was enraged, and promptly banished him from his home, and forbade all to assist him at peril of the Duke's displeasure."

"Ah, poor Alreid. I was afraid such might happen to him."

"Yes. Well, it was a sad and disheveled young man that stood in my hall after he requested an audience with me. He sought to secure my forgiveness, he said, after having caused me such pain. Knowing what you would have wanted, I did forgive him and offered him sanctuary in my home. I have never cared for his father very much, you know."

"And now?"

"Having no other task for him and knowing that he needed to be occupied with some work, I set him to ordering my library. Don't think I don't see that smile, my son...I know that my library was neglected for years, and was badly in need of a willing caretaker. And so he has become, and blossomed in the doing. I believe he has found himself in the midst of all those dusty old tomes, and is finally somewhat happy."

"Mother, you are a wonder. You constantly amaze me, and I love you for it."

"Then surely, when all this is done, you will find time for a small visit to your mother's home, no? Not to stay, of course; I would not ask that. Merely a sort of...how do you say?...a vacation, yes? Bring all your brothers and come for a visit."

"That we can do, and it is most gracious of you to ask. But there is another thing I must speak to you of, as well. I know that you are familiar with Braewynn's doings here in the human realms, and the evil which he has visited upon many who are too young and innocent to protect themselves. It is my hope that we will, upon my victory, come into possession of many of those he has coerced and corrupted. It may be that there will be many children in need of succor who have been badly damaged and traumatized; too many for us to care for here in our small house. I would, thus, ask a boon of you: that you open the doors of the manor at Agryvaine to them, and assist in their recovery. I do not know how many we will find and assist, but it could be only a few, or a great many. I do not know yet the full extent of his business ventures, but I fear the worst."

Elenore's response was immediate. "Granted, my son. The full resources of Agryvaine shall be at the disposal of these children – healers of both body and mind, and whatever else they shall need. Nothing shall be held back, I assure you. And now, my son, I believe we are out of time. The hour is upon us, if you would arrive in good order at the dueling grounds."

(12)

It was a long and very quiet drive to Enumclaw, with Ralph behind the wheel of the old Volvo, and Sandy riding shotgun. Peter and I sat in the back seat, each of us caught up on our own thoughts and not saying much. The Lady had told us that she would provide her own transportation to the site, and would meet us there on our arrival. Unlike Sandy, Ralph was a calm and graceful driver, and the Volvo seemed to fairly hum under his hand.

All too soon, we exited the freeway and headed into the tiny town of Enumclaw, tooling along through its quiet and deserted streets. We were traveling a lot faster than speed limit, and Ralph had asked me to do "We're not here," duty until we exited the other side of town. It must have worked – though we passed a couple of police cars, not one seemed to pay us the slightest mind.

And then we were there. We left the small, blacktopped road with its infrequent streetlights, and turned into a narrow dirt road with deep potholes. The Volvo negotiated the dirt track easily, jouncing along and creaking, but still willing. At one point I felt the tingle of wards, but weakly. A little later, I felt it again, this time much stronger.

We left the cover of the trees, and a large clearing opened up ahead of us. There was a bonfire burning in the center of the meadow, and a number of cars parked around it. I had an impression of many people standing and milling about, but it was hard to make out individuals.

We pulled up, and Ralph set the parking brake and cut the engine. There was a moment of silence, and then Sandy shrugged as if to say "Well, here we go," opened the door and got out of the car. The rest of us piled out and almost without thinking formed up behind him, presenting a solid front to the rest of the those in the field. And, now that I could see clearly, there were quite a lot of them here. They seemed to be split into two distinct camps, with the great bonfire at the dividing point.

On the far side of the fire, a small pavilion had been set up – a simple framework with a central peak and samite draped down to just below the point where the walls began, with a woven groundcloth to cover the dirt. Within this open structure, Torrel and Daindraen and two others stood and waited for us. The other two, clad in formal robes similar in cut but colored black and red instead of the white and gold of the Lios Alfar, stood silently and watched us approach.

"Be welcome, Sandellifer of Agryvaine and companions." Daindraen's voice was gravelly and deep. Then turning to one of the Drow that stood silently next to him, "The champion for Seelie is arrived, Danthel, and the hour is upon us. Where is your champion?"

"Patience, Daindraen. He arrives even as we speak," the Unseelie representative answered. "See how he comes even now."

And shining on the darkened wall of trees, headlights could be seen approaching along the dirt road that we had driven just moments before. In moments, the black BMW sedan that I remembered so well pulled up alongside our old Volvo wagon and stopped in a small cloud of dust. The engine purred for a moment and then cut off, and the driver's door opened to reveal Arturo, clad in immaculate evening dress. He stepped to the back door and opened it, and Braewynn stepped out. He was dressed in the traditional finery of an Unseelie noble – close fitting black and silver, with a half cloak covering his back and one arm. When they had crossed the short distance from the car to the pavilion, Danthel spoke again: "Welcome Braewynn, champion of the Unseelie, and your second." He bowed to them both, and Braewynn nodded to the Unseelie Honor Court representative.

There was a moment of silence, and then Torrel stepped away from us and gestured Sandy forward, even as the other Drow did the same with Braewynn.

"Ladies and Gentles of the courts, I present to you Sandellifer, heir apparent of Agryvaine and the accuser in this case. He lays charges of dishonor and insult to his clan brother against his opponent, and would prove the verity of his claim on the field of honor, in mortal combat." His voice, without seeming to be raised, penetrated to the far end of the field, and raised a storm of cheering from the Seelie side of the crowd of spectators.

When the cheering had died down, Danthel stepped forward with Braewynn at his heels. "Ladies and Gentles of the courts, I present to you Braewynn, Duke of Athelon, who is accused in this case. He denies any wrongdoing and would prove his innocence of the charges laid against him in this case on the field of honor, in mortal combat." Immediately a great roar of cheering rose from the Unseelie spectators, and Braewynn nodded briskly in acknowledgment.

Both the champions and the Honor Court representatives returned to the small pavilion, and Daindraen stepped forward.

"Both combatants shall have ten minutes, as they are reckoned here in the human lands, to prepare for combat. At that time, the contest shall commence. Go, and return with your seconds at the appointed time."

Dismissed for the moment, both men turned and retreated to their respective vehicles followed by their seconds: Ralph as Sandy's second, and Arturo walking behind Braewynn.

In the lurid, red light cast by the bonfire, I could see both of them near their respective cars, stripping out of their clothes and being assisted into their combat gear – Braewynn into dark leathers, and Sandy into bright, silver ring mail. When both were fully dressed, each of the seconds went to the trunk of the respective cars; Arturo pulled a long, narrow box from the boot of the BMW, and Ralph returned from his trip to the back of the Volvo with a similar package.

Carefully setting the dark wooden box on the hood of the Beemer, Arturo opened the wooden lid to reveal twin rapiers nestled in velvet within. He withdrew each and handed it slowly to Braewynn, who placed them in scabbards at his belt and checked to make sure their draw was clean and unimpeded.

Meanwhile, Ralph set the oak box he was carrying on the hood of the Volvo, and popped open the lid. I saw his face go momentarily blue with the light from inside the box, and he reached in and pulled out Kaldor. It was a long, heavy looking two-handed sword, with a great cabochon sapphire set in the pommel, but otherwise a very workman-like blade: the hilt was wrapped in leather, and it had plain brass quilons. Its blade was perfectly straight, double- edged and unadorned. He laid it across his forearm with his other hand on the crossguard and offered the hilt to Sandy, who took it from him with a smile. The moment it felt its master's hand, a tiny rill of blue fire ran down the length of the blade and burned at the tip for a moment. Without even looking, Sandy hefted it and slid it into a baldric across his back, the hilt standing up from behind his right shoulder. Finally, each of the seconds bowed to their duelist, and followed them back to the pavilion.

When they stood once more in front of the Honor Court representatives from each court, Danthen spoke again. "Each of you is familiar with the terms of this challenge. There will be no quarter given – the duel will continue until one or both of you lies dead, by your own consents. Are each of you fully prepared?"

"Aye," Sandy said.

"I am prepared," Braewynn replied.

"Then the combatants will repair to the field, and the duel commence."

Both men walked slowly to a space on the far side of the bonfire, with the Honor Court marshals following. When they stood ready, Torrel called out, "Combatants, salute."

Kaldor cleared the baldric in an arc of blue light, sweeping down and then up to stand upright before Sandy's face, and then back down and to the right. "Beware, my enemy. I would have your life for your crimes." Sandy's voice was low and dangerous, not meant for the ears of the spectators.

Braewynn sneered and raised one rapier in a cursory salute. "Come and take it then, if you can. As the father, so the son."

"Combatants, begin." No sooner had the command been given then both of the men glided forward, almost too fast for the eye to follow, and there was a sudden explosion of sound – the crash-slither of sword on sword as each sought a way through the other's guard.

It all happened much to fast for me to know what was really happening. I don't know much about dueling or sword fighting, so to me it looked like a blur as each rained a flurry of strokes on the other and parried in between – and while – attacking. I glanced over at Torrel and Daindraen, and both watched with intense interest. I thought they were probably following every stroke and seeing both the combatant's strategies, and I was a little envious.

When I glanced back, I noticed that Braewynn was backing slowly and Sandy was advancing, but I also noticed that Braewynn was always moving in a sideways direction, looking for an unprotected flank while Sandy moved in opposition, always presenting his most solid defense.

With a sudden screeling of blade on blade, Sandy knocked aside one of the rapiers, parried a thrust from the second, and slipped Kaldor's tip inside Braewynn's guard to trace a tiny line on the Drow's face. Blood immediately began to drip from the cut, and Braewynn grinned ferally and sped up his attacks, rapiers striking like vipers, probing for a chance to wound in return. I was astonished when Kaldor met every attack and turned it. How could anyone move so fast?

I glanced away again, just a brief, questioning look at Ralph. He caught the look and leaned forward.

"He's good," he murmured. "I think he could beat me, and I'm no slouch. I don't know if he's good enough to beat Sandy, though. I have a feeling we'll soon find out."

Two minutes later, we did find out. The end, when it came, happened far too fast for me to see what actually took place. One moment they were each a blur of deadly movement, the next Braewynn was down, lying on his back in the dirty grass of the pasture with one rapier fallen from his hand, the other pinned beneath his own fallen body. Kaldor's tip hovered menacingly at his throat, a hairs-breadth from the deadly stroke that would end the contest. One breath, one heartbeat and we'd won!

But the moment never came. As Sandy stepped back slightly, Braewynn scrambled to his knees, head hanging and his shoulders slumped in defeat. He left both rapiers on the ground and knelt before his enemy. But even as he came to his knees, a slight movement of his right hand produced a dagger in that hand, a dagger with a dull grey blade edged in black, as if it were tarnished. His movement to his knees became a desperate lunge forward, the dagger striking up and forward to bury itself to the hilt in Sandy's thigh, ripping through the ring mail that should have protected him as if it were tin foil.

The effect was immediate. Sandy went white as a sheet, the glow of his armor was snuffed out like a candle, and he staggered back, then fell to his knees. He gripped the dagger, but his hands kept slipping and he couldn't pull it out. Braewynn slowly got to his feet and leaned down to pick up his rapiers, no longer in a hurry. There was a dead silence on the field.

I didn't notice much of this though, because the second Braewynn attacked with the dagger, two things happened to me: first, there was a surge of heat in my right front pocket where I carried the pouch I had been given all those days ago. The second was the voice of Elenore speaking in my mind, her voice stern and commanding.

"Now is the moment, young Bryon. The boon is come due – reach into your pocket and take in hand that which you find in the pouch!"

I didn't question, even for a moment. With feverish haste I wrenched the pouch out of my pocket, noticing in passing a glow of red from the pursed end of the pouch where it was drawn up

166

with a leather thong. I stripped open the top and shook the pouch over my open palm, and a glowing red stone, about the size of a hen's egg, dropped into my hand. I closed my fingers around it, and suddenly I went away.

I was standing in gray, swirling mist. There was nothing around me; I couldn't tell how far I could see because it was all flat and featureless. From somewhere far away I could feel Dubhain's desperate efforts to find me, but he was lost and defeated by the fog.

"Welcome, Bryon. I cannot tell you what a relief it is to see another after all the long years."

I turned to see who was talking to me, and there was a man of the Lios Alfar standing there behind me, watching me. He was tall, and his hair was bright red, hanging down his back in a long, thick braid. He was dressed in elven plate armor, and a longsword hung at his side in a gemmed scabbard.

"What... no, who... Oh, hell with it. What do you need from me?"

The elf threw his head back and laughed. "I know the feeling, Bryon. Events have moved very quickly, haven't they? I am Tyliran, once the husband of Lady Sigrid, whom you know as Elenore, and father of Sandellifer."

I gaped at him for a moment, taking all that in. "Once the husband? What happened to you? Why are you in this place?"

"I'm dead, Bryon. I was murdered during the Great War – taken from behind by Braewynn while I knelt to heal a fallen comrade, and slain by the very same blade that even now kills my son. Only the quick action of my very dear wife saved my spirit from its hunger, and placed me within the gem, where we are now. I have been here just a bit over a thousand years, but now… well, with your kind permission, my wait is at an end."

"What was that dagger, anyway? It shouldn't have been able to do that to Sandy."

"We have little time, Bryon. Though time flows differently here, and all this happens in but a fraction of the time it would take in the outer world, yet still time passes. But to answer your question – its name is Dragontooth, and it is made of cold iron. It is absolutely deadly to any of our kind, for it feeds on magic and spirit. Sandellifer has very little time, if we would save him."

"You can save Sandy?"

"I can. I will, and avenge my own death in the same stroke."

"But the oaths? I didn't think you could…"

"I am unbound – dead before any oaths were sworn."

"Then do it. What do you need?"

"I need to borrow your body for a time. I hope I can return it unharmed, but one never knows."

"Just do it."

He grinned fiercely, and the next thing I knew, I was back in the world, and set aside in my own mind, watching from the sidelines. I could see that I was dressed suddenly in the same elven plate armor that Tyliran had worn, and the same narrow, straight, longsword hung at my waist.

I spun and ripped the sword from the scabbard, even as I threw my head back and howled "Braewynn!"

I watched as my body, firmly under Tyliran's control, ran with impossible grace across the clearing toward the Drow, sword coming up and back for an annihilating blow.

Braewynn turned shocked eyes on me as I flowed to the attack. Even in his surprise he reacted quickly, both rapiers coming up to en guarde. One sweeping blow from the longsword sheared through both the blades, leaving the Drow holding nothing but two hilts with a stub of blade sticking out of each. His mouth fell open in shock, but he didn't have time for even a word as the longsword whipped around with blinding speed and slammed forward through his chest. A single word from the spirit that used my body, and an explosion of fire swept through the blade and raged through the Drow's impaled body, raising the dark elf up onto his toes. For a brief moment, the bones of his face and skull shone brightly beneath his skin, limned in raging fire, and a gout of flames burst from his mouth. Then he slumped back, sliding off the bright, silvron blade and falling limply to the grass.

"A thousand years I have waited for that moment. The cur is dead, and now we must save my son." Tyliran's voice was calm, but I could feel the underlying urgency. "We haven't much time; a thousand years of waiting, and now I am defeated by seconds." With the same speed as I had run to the attack, I slammed the sword back into the scabbard and strode to where Sandy's limp body lay sprawled on the damp grass, one hand lying limply on his thigh where the dark dagger stood out of his flesh.

Lady Sigrid already knelt on the other side of him, and I went to my knees across from her, our faces a scant foot apart.

"Tyliran, it consumes him and I cannot stop it. Ysendin strives with all its might, and it is not enough. It consumes all the magic I attempt – how should we proceed?"

"Lady wife, I cannot heal this wound. No, do not despair! Though I cannot heal it, I can delay it. My magic is greater, and it knows my spirit of old. Even now it reaches for me, and I will not deny it. Perhaps, with enough time, another can heal what I cannot."

With that, he reached my hand down, touched the black iron crossguard where it lay against the flesh of his son, and began to feed himself to the blade. I could feel its ravening, endless hunger beginning to siphon off his spirit, and how he resisted its pull to give himself a few moments more time, and the agony it caused him.

"You have been more brave and generous than I have had any reason to expect, young Bryon. There is a thing that I would do for you, in reward. I see that you do not know the path of Oneness with your horsebrother, and I would show it to you. All of your kind must be shown by an older mentor at an early age, and since you had none, I must suffice. Watch, and see the way."

He made a tiny adjustment in my mind, and suddenly it was there, like a shining path through my thoughts. Of course! It was so easy – why hadn't I seen it for myself? As I was studying it, I felt the last of his spirit drain away into the dagger, and I found myself back in control of my body. He was gone, utterly consumed. I stared across Sandy's body at Lady Sigrid, watched in astonishment as she leaned forward and placed her hand on the dagger, saw her stiffen as she began to feed herself to the blade in willing sacrifice, and then -

"No. This shall not be, sister. Not all need die." I'd been so focused on Lady Sigrid that I hadn't seen the arrival of the two who stood behind her, outlined against the bright light of the bonfire. The stranger on the right was a woman of the Lios Alfar, tall and fair, terrible in her beauty, and radiating magical might as I'd never seen before. To the left, next to her, stood a Drow woman, dark and beautiful, radiant in a nimbus of power the equal of the first. Without even glancing around to see every knee on the field bent to the two of them, I knew who they were.

"My lady queen, can you save him?"

Without answering Sigrid's question directly, Gloriana turned to the Drow beside her. "Hail, Maeve. It has been long since last we met, sister. Would you assist in a healing, as once we did so long ago?"

Maeve stared down at the scene before her for a moment, her dark eyes measuring each of us. She paused, then said "This young knight has given me a very neat solution to a thorny problem. Yon carrion heap -" and here she gestured with graceful disdain at Braewynn's body, "had violated the laws of Unseelie, and drawn attention to us here in the human realm. I warned him, but he heeded me not. Perchance I shall assist, as reward for the convenience this young knight has afforded me. Heal him then, Gloriana, and I shall lend strength as it is needed."

Immediately Gloriana's hand shot forward and hovered over the hilt of the dagger, and she began a quiet chant of closing and containing, of withdrawal. Maeve reached a hand out and laid it on the other Queen's shoulder, and she began to sing a descant to Gloriana's song, and the slowly building nimbus of power around the Queen of Seelie brightened, flowing down her hand and centering on the dark knife.

Slowly, very slowly and resisting mightily, the blade began to relinquish its hold. After long, tense minutes it slid out of Sandy's thigh and hovered over him, and when the tip left his flesh, a gout of black, foul-smelling fluid poured from the rent in his skin, pouring down to pool on the grass beneath and instantly killing it.

"It is a foul thing, is it not? Even now it strives to return and consume him. It is an evil all its own, and it has murdered many over the long centuries. I think its time should end, Maeve."

"Aye, sister. I do not believe we can, of our own power, destroy it. But perhaps we may send it to a place even it cannot resist. I believe the great heat at the heart of the sun would overwhelm it."

"Your skill is greater than mine own in that area, Maeve. Of your courtesy, if you would be kind enough?"

"Right gladly. And no sooner said than done."

One moment the dagger hung suspended, and the next it was gone. I didn't feel its extinction in the sun, but Maeve looked grimly pleased, and Gloriana relieved.

"Now then, a bit of healing and the deed is done. Since he is one of yours, and your gift of healing is greater than mine own, I will assist and marvel at your skill, sister." Maeve smiled teasingly at Gloriana, seemingly perfectly at ease. Gloriana smiled back, and held her hand out once again, this time over the ugly, blackened hole in Sandy's thigh.

As she began again to chant, the lips of the wound – at first peeled back and blackened as though severely burned – began to lighten in color and draw back together. Torn muscle, abraded bone and shredded tendons began to knit, writhing in an ecstasy of regeneration and re-growth. It took only a few minutes, and the wound closed and the skin healed, leaving only a line of pink scar tissue to show that it had ever existed.

While all this was happening, I had slid back until I was nearly sitting on Ralph and Peter's feet, still on my knees and watching intently. Lady Sigrid had not moved, remaining at Sandy's side with her head bowed, watching the wound heal.

Now she rose to her feet and bowed deeply to her queen, and then turned and bowed only slightly less deeply to the queen of Unseelie.

"I have no words to express my gratitude, my Lady. Both I and House Agryvaine stand in your debt for the aid that you have rendered to us this day." Though tears stood on her pale cheeks, Sigrid radiated pride and dignity as she addressed the queen of the the rival court.

"Nonsense, dear Lady. I have known the special agony that the death of a child brings, and would not wish such on any. Had I acted more swiftly once before, my own child might still be with me. That aside, this young knight has done me a service, though he knew it not. I still owe him for that beyond a mere assist with healing, and so here is the resolve of my heart: all the former Duke of Athelon's holdings are hereby forfeit to the Crown. I cede all of those holdings that exist in the human realms to yon knight, Sandellifer, to hold and dispose of as he sees fit. Further, I have ordered all the children the late Duke had congress with to be gathered and held in a central place, with appropriate guards. I understand that you will be responsible for their recovery, Lady Sigrid. I want them to disappear. I do not wish to revisit this issue. Are we agreed? Yes? Then all debt between us is discharged, and perhaps you will think a bit less harshly of the Queen of Unseelie in the future, no?" Even in the deep formality of the moment, the irrepressible and sly smile of the Dark Queen shone momentarily, and Sigrid smiled wanly and nodded.

"As you will it, Lady, so let it be."

"Even so, Lady Sigrid. Do not delay in taking charge of your new wards, Lady. They are many, and I fear that the guardians I set over them may grow…hmm, restless." And again the Dark Lady's smile shone out, tinged with just a hint of malice. "Then I feel that we are finished here, are we not, Gloriana? Really, my sister, we must meet when there is not a crisis at hand…but perhaps not too soon, eh?" And with a bow of her head to her sister sovereign and to Lady Sigrid, she turned and walked away, back to the Unseelie side of the pavilion, and then disappeared with a wave of her hand.

When the dark Queen had disappeared, it seemed that Sigrid reached the end of her strength. She seemed to slump a little, and tears began to roll down her cheeks to fall on the bodice of her blue and white gown, now stained and muddy at the knees where she had knelt on the grass.

"Come sister, all is well. Disaster has been averted, and your son lives and will thrive once again." Gloriana stepped forward and enfolded Lady Sigrid in a deep and long hug, holding her head to her shoulder. After a long moment, she released her hold and stepped back, but laid her hand along Sigrid's cheek. "It has ever been your way to hold all inside you, Sigrid. Pain, joy, grief and pleasure cannot be denied and contained forever, and you must release them. Know that your steadfast loyalty and support is never taken for granted, and that when I am wearied by the travails of court, you are a bright place in my thoughts. Would that I had the pleasure of your presence in my court more often, but I shall not command it, only ask it by your leave. It would be a comfort to me."

"My Lady, you shall have it, as you have already, to the least and last measure, all my loyalty and faith."

"Those, as Queen, I command. But I would have not just your loyalty and faith, but your friendship, and that is beyond my command. That is what I would ask for in greater measure, Lady. I hope that it may be so." She gazed long and deeply into Lady Sigrid's eyes, and then smiled. "I, too, must take my leave. I hope to see you again and soon, dear friend."

She turned then, and waved to Torrel and Daindraen. "My lords, attend. We must return to court. Farewell, Sigrid. Take care of your son." And then, she disappeared.

(13)

"…and then we loaded you into the back of the Volvo like a sack of potatoes, drove you home and put you to bed. And that was all there was to it." I smiled at Sandy and crossed my arms across my chest. "It wasn't a big deal, really."

Sandy smiled back, a little weakly. He was still pretty under the weather, trying to recover from his wound. Despite the healing he had undergone, it still hurt a lot even though he tried to cover for it.

"Let me see if I've got it right, ok? First I was stabbed with a knife that is virtually invariably fatal to anyone it comes into contact with, then the ghost of my father possessed you and you killed Braewynn, then the queens of both Seelie AND Unseelie showed up, removed the knife and healed me. And then my mother cried."

"Yup, that about sums it up."

"And that's no big deal?"

"Nope."

"Damn, I sure hope I'm never around when something you consider a big deal happens."

"Me neither." For a moment I was able to keep a straight face, but then I couldn't hold it. A big grin broke loose and pasted itself right across my face – I couldn't help it, I was just so glad to see him awake and feeling better. I did have one question for him, though.

"Sandy, how did your father defeat Braewynn so easily? It took every bit of your skill, but he trashed him in two hits."

"Well, you know the longsword he wore? It's name is Chryssand, and it was made for the Great War, not for dueling. Both Kaldor and Braewynn's rapiers are weapons designed for dueling, and they don't have the spells on them that the great weapons from the war did. Compared to Chryssand, Kaldor is like a stick." He paused for a moment and then asked a question of his own. "So you and Dubhain...?"

"Yup, right after we put you in bed and everyone got a little sleep."

"And that was ok?"

"Oh, much better than ok. It's frikkin' amazing, Sandy. Here, watch this!" I closed my eyes for a moment, and when I opened them again, they blazed solid, pupil-less yellow. Looking at him with Dubhain's vision, I could still see the dark blot on his thigh, but every other part of him shone right through the blankets on the bed – a rich, deep golden flow of energy. I'd never realized that Dubhain saw energy, not bodies. It was just one of the benefits of our newly conjoined existence.

"Oh, nice. That's going to make a hell of an impression at Halloween."

"Yeah…I was thinking of going as a vampire, you know. There's a few people out there that I owe a little scare."

"Bryon, don't even think about it."

"Kidding! I was kidding…mostly."

"You better be. Now, what did you bring me?"

I reached over and dragged the night stand even closer to the bed, and began stacking my offerings on it. "Let's see…Vogue magazine, two novels, CDs from downstairs that Peter says you like, couple sodas, and one of Peter's special sandwiches. Anything else you need? No? Well, I'll leave you to it then. Call my cell if you need anything, ok?"

Already reading the cover of the Vogue magazine, Sandy waved as I walked out of the room and headed down to the kitchen for my own lunch.

ABOUT THE AUTHOR

Andrew James lives and writes in the Pacific Northwest, sharing a house with his best friends and three miniature daschunds.